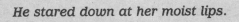

He stared down at her moist lips.

They looked so soft, so vulnerable, and without thinking, he bent his head and placed a gentle kiss against them. His only intent had been to comfort her, but the feel of her warm mouth beneath his destroyed that fiction, and he was soon kissing her with the fierce passion he had been denying since the first moment he saw her.

Maggie felt his passion and answered it with her own shy desire. Ian was the only comfort in a world suddenly fraught with danger, and she clung to him with a strength born of desperation.

All the lectures he had given his agents over the years about the dangers of becoming involved while on a mission flew from his head, and for the first time in more than a decade he allowed his emotions free reign. . .

Also by Joan E. Overfield
Published by Fawcett Books:

HER LADYSHIP'S MAN

BRIDE'S LEAP

Joan E. Overfield

FAWCETT CREST • NEW YORK

In memory of Sister C and the Upward Bound Program, who taught me there is nothing we can't achieve if only we try.

Prologue

"A holiday? Now? My God, Marchfield, have you taken leave of your senses?" Sir's sea blue eyes glittered with indignation as he glared at the dark-haired man sitting at his bedside. "The czar and his court will be arriving within a month; I can hardly go traipsing off to Bath to take the waters like some damned invalid!"

"I don't see why not," Anthony Selton, the Duke of Marchfield, replied with his usual aplomb. "With Boney safely caged on Elba, things have been rather quiet, and in any case, I should think you could do with a dose of Bath's restorative waters." His ice gray eyes rested pointedly on the thick bandages wrapped around the other man's shoulders.

"A mere trifle," Sir grumbled, silently cursing the prince for sending him to Marchfield's country seat to recover from his wounds. He disliked being vulnerable in any fashion, and despite his fondness for the duke and his impish wife, he would have preferred holing up in the privacy of his rooms until he had regained his strength. Lord knew he had done it enough times in the past, he thought, his lips thinning in displeasure.

"Had that 'trifle' been an inch or two lower, we wouldn't be having this conversation," Anthony said, his keen glance catching Sir's small grimace. "Dr. Hamilton is amazed the bullet missed your heart and lungs, and he says it will be several weeks before you will be yourself again."

"I heard him, but it changes nothing. It is imperative that I be in Dover by week's end, and I'll be damned if I'll let a musketball stop me!" Sir snapped, thrusting his good hand through his thick blond hair. It had been four days since he and three of his agents were ambushed in the small cove, and he was champing at the bit to be after the men he suspected of betraying them. He knew there were several men in his organization, Anthony included, who were more than capable of tracking the traitors down, but it had been *his* mission that had gone awry, and he would not rest until he had apprehended those he held responsible.

Anthony leaned back in his chair, regarding his superior with a grim look. He had worked with Sir long enough to know how he would rail at the very suggestion that he set aside his duties merely because he was wounded, but the prince's instructions had been explicit.

"I am afraid you have no say in the matter," he said bluntly, deciding it would be best to make a clean breast of it. "The suggestion that you take a few weeks holiday isn't entirely my own."

Sir closed his eyes, a blistering curse forming soundlessly on his lips. Even though he had been expecting something like this, the reality of it struck him almost as painfully as had the sniper's bullet. He gave a heavy sigh and then opened his eyes, his expression cold as he studied Marchfield's face. "The prince?"

Anthony nodded. "And I must say that I agree with him. You have driven yourself hard these last few years, and His Highness and I both feel it would be best for the organization if you take a brief leave. Admit it, Sir," he added when Sir opened his lips in protest, "if this was some other man we were discussing, you know you would insist that he rest."

Sir glared at the duke. "Damn it, Anthony, but you fight in a most underhanded manner! Is there nothing you won't do to achieve your objective?"

"No." Anthony gave him a warm smile. "But then, I have learned from the best. The first thing you taught me is that the end always justifies the means."

Before Sir could attempt a reply, the door to the bedroom opened, and a dark-haired woman with a babe held in her arms entered the room. "Ah, good, you are awake," Jacinda, the Duchess of Marchfield, said, her hazel eyes sparkling with satisfaction as she saw him sitting up. "I have brought your namesake in to see you. You have been shockingly neglectful in your duties as a godfather."

"My apologies, ma'am," Sir answered, studying the child with a wary expression. He had little to do with children as a rule, and couldn't remember ever seeing one so young.

"Well, have you told Sir you are to take his place while he is away?" Jacinda asked, her eyes going to her husband's face as she took the chair he had just vacated.

Anthony shot his wife an exasperated look before turning to Sir. "I told her nothing," he promised the other man, "but you know her regrettably sharp ears. A pity her mind is not nearly half so sharp," he added with a threatening scowl, "otherwise she wouldn't be blurting out things she should not."

"Oh, pooh!" Jacinda sniffed, lifting the baby to her shoulder and patting its tiny back. "As it happens, I didn't hear a thing. It simply makes sense to me. Sir can hardly be expected to go on as he has, and that means that as his second, you will assume command." She gave Sir a dimpled smile. "Where will you be taking your holiday, Sir? With your family?"

"Bath has been suggested," Anthony said, keeping a wary eye on his friend. "There is a house we sometimes use, and—"

"No," Sir interrupted, his face taking on a stony look that was all too familiar to Anthony. "His Highness might order me to take a holiday, but I'll be hanged if I'll let him dictate the terms. I have a small cottage in Cornwall, and that is where I shall go." He glared at Jacinda as if daring her to disagree.

"Cornwall sounds quite delightful," Jacinda replied, inclining her head in approval. "The warm sea breeze will do you wonders, and while you are there, perhaps you might give some thought to finding a bride. With the war all but ended, it is time you were settling down."

Such high-handed meddling on top of the prince's orders made Sir's jaw clench in anger. "The fighting might well be over, but the war is far from 'ended,' " he informed her in his stiffest tone. "And I will thank you, Your Grace, not to interfere in my private affairs."

Jacinda wrinkled her nose at him. "Now I know you are angry with me," she said with total unconcern. "You only address me by my title when you are up in the boughs. But for your information, Sir, I was only trying to help. You are my husband's dearest friend; is it not surprising I should wish to see you happily situated?"

Sir glared at her for a moment longer, and then

4

his mouth softened into a reluctant smile. "Baggage," he accused her ruefully, his eyes flicking to the duke, who was regarding his wife with affectionate amusement. "However do you endure such an apeleader, Marchfield? 'Tis a wonder to me that you haven't throttled her by now."

"The thought has crossed my mind," Anthony replied in a languid fashion, his eyes resting on his wife's face, "but I fear it would be somewhat difficult to explain to the children. For some unknown reason, they seem inordinately fond of their recalcitrant mama."

While Jacinda responded indignantly to her husband's teasing, Sir's mind drifted to the subject of his forced leave. What a pack of nonsense, he thought, his expression growing bleak at the prospect of spending several weeks doing nothing more strenuous than watching the weeds grow in his garden. He should go mad, and really it was all so unnecessary. He knew his abilities better than any man, and he knew the bullet wound in his shoulder wouldn't keep him down for more than a week. Yet what else could he do? The prince was his superior, and much as he might rebel at the notion, an order was still an order.

"How will you be traveling to Cornwall, Sir?" Anthony had taken the baby from his wife and was cuddling him against his chest. "We have a new carriage that has never been used, and we should be more than happy to place it at your disposal."

Sir considered the duke's offer before shaking his head. "No, thank you, Marchfield, but I shall take the mail coach, as I usually do."

"Nonsense." Jacinda glowered at him. "We have over four carriages gathering dust in our stables, and it is perfectly foolish for you to submit yourself to an overcrowded, badly sprung carriage when we—"

"The mail coach," Sir repeated, his tone brooking no opposition. "And I shall leave tomorrow."

Jacinda continued glaring at him. "You are behaving as childishly as Tony!" she accused crossly.

Sir's lips quirked in a half smile. "Perhaps."

Jacinda threw up her hands in a gesture of disgust. "Well, will you at least be careful?" she asked, studying Sir with a mixture of anger and concern.

"Being careful is always my intention, Your Grace," he replied, the sparkle in his eyes belying his grave tones. "Besides, I am only going to Cornwall, and I have it on the best authority that nothing untoward ever happens in Cornwall. You may rest assured that other than expiring from boredom, I shall be in no danger whatsoever. You have my word on it."

Chapter One

"What do you mean my carriage isn't here?" Miss Margaret Chambers demanded, her dark gray eyes narrowing in fury as she glared at the hapless innkeeper standing before her. "My solicitor assured me there would be a coach and four waiting for me on the fifteenth of the month. This *is* The Royal Spaniard, is it not?"

"Y-yes, miss, so 'tis," the innkeeper stammered, nervously dabbing at his forehead with the edge of his grimy apron. "But I know naught of what you're sayin'. The mail coach will be stoppin' here tomorrow, though, and I'm sure you and the other lady should have no trouble bookin' passage." His dark eyes flicked admiringly towards the diminutive blonde standing beside Maggie.

"The mail coach?" Maggie repeated, strongly tempted to stamp her foot in a fit of childish temper. She'd been so looking forward to arriving at Bride's Leap in a manner befitting the new owner, and the thought of arriving on the mail coach like a bolt of drapery material quite cast her into the sulks. There had to be something she could do, she thought, her russet-colored eyebrows meeting in a frown.

"Is there a private coach I might hire?" she asked, brightening at the sudden thought. Her former employer, Mrs. Graft, had often traveled in this fashion, and although Maggie disliked aping the disagreeable woman in any fashion, the situation was a desperate one. Of what use was a hundred thousand pounds if it couldn't provide a few creature comforts? she reasoned.

The innkeeper shook his head. "There not be a private coach between here and London what is to be let," he said, his tone apologetic. "The only thing I can offer you and your companion is my two best rooms. Other than that . . ." He shrugged his beefy shoulders.

Maggie bit back a retort that would have had Mrs. Graft swooning in horror. As the daughter of a colonel, she had spent a lifetime following the drum, and she had learned early on to take what life handed her. Like it or not, it appeared they would have to pass the night at the inn.

"Very well, Mr. Pruitt," she said, extracting a gold coin from her reticule and sliding it across the sticky surface of the counter, "we shall take the rooms. I'd also like to hire a private parlor, if I might. I dislike eating in my room," she added, remembering all those times she was banished to her small bedchamber while Mrs. Graft entertained her guests.

The coin disappeared into the proprietor's huge fist. "I've only got but the one parlor, miss, and it is already bespoken by a Captain Sherrill. But I'm sure he'd not be objectin' to sharin' with you ladies once I explains things to 'im."

Wise now to the ways of the world, Maggie passed him a second coin, and within a matter of minutes, she and her companion, Miss Constance Spenser, were being shown into their rooms. After the effusive innkeeper had departed, Maggie collapsed onto her bed with a resigned sigh.

"What next, Constance?" she asked, contemplating the water-stained ceiling wearily. "These past few weeks have been nothing but one trial after another, and if I were the suspicious sort of female, I vow I would think there was some dreadful conspiracy against me!"

"Why, Miss Chambers, whatever can you mean?" Constance asked, her blue eyes widening as she turned to Maggie.

Maggie hid a smile at her companion's reaction. Constance had been in her employ a little over two months, and it was obvious that she had been tenderly sheltered. She was a lady to her fingertips, and Maggie often had the impression the other woman disapproved of her blunt and occasionally flippant manner. Ah well, she shrugged mentally, the girl was young and would soon learn. This was only her first position, after all.

"I mean, Constance, that I am starting to feel rather like Job; beset by plague and pestilence," she answered, her gray eyes twinkling as she rose to her feet and began exploring the small room.

"Surely you are exaggerating, Miss Chambers," Constance reproved in her gentle voice, turning her attention to the portmanteau the footman had brought into the room. "You will forgive my bluntness, I am sure, but there are many who would not consider inheriting a substantial fortune a 'plague.'"

"That is so." Maggie conceded the point with a light laugh as she bent to help Constance. After so many years laboring for her daily bread, she was still unaccustomed to sitting idle while others worked about her, and she took pleasure in performing the small task. "But even you must agree that of late, I seem to attract disaster the way one of Mr. Franklin's rods attracts lightning."

"If you are referring to that unfortunate incident at the ruins, you must acknowledge that you aren't exactly blameless," Constance pointed out with a tiny smile. "The grounds keeper did warn you that staircase was unstable."

"Yes, but he didn't say the whole thing would collapse beneath me and leave me dangling like a ripe plum," Maggie said, scowling at the memory of the accident that had occurred less than a sennight ago. She and Constance had been happily exploring a particularly decrepit part of the ancient Norman keep when the rotting staircase suddenly gave way beneath her feet. She still shuddered as she remembered the horror she had felt clinging to the banister a good twenty feet above the stone floor.

"Thank heaven that kind man and his brother were there to hear your cries," Constance said, sending Maggie a sweet smile. "Otherwise I fear you would have had a nasty fall."

"You mean I'd have broken my neck," Maggie retorted with her customary frankness. "And what about that bookcase at Mr. Bigley's?" she demanded, recalling her latest mishap. "You cannot claim it was unstable!"

"No," Constance agreed, her dark blond lashes sweeping over her eyes to hide the laughter. "But you were climbing it at the time, and that's doubtlessly why it toppled over on you."

"Well, there was no ladder, and I'd never seen Homer printed in the original Greek." Maggie defended her actions with an embarrassed grumble. "Besides, I hadn't climbed that far, barely three shelves, and I hardly weigh enough to have brought the whole thing crashing down on me. If that volume of Milton hadn't struck me in the forehead and alerted me to the danger, I should have been squashed like a beetle. And they say the classics have no redeeming value."

Constance ignored Maggie's teasing jibe. "Please don't even joke about it," she implored, casting Maggie a worried look. "You really don't think someone is plotting against you . . . do you?"

Maggie tilted her head to one side as she considered the matter. In the two months since unexpectedly inheriting her Great-Uncle Ellsworth's fortune, her life had changed dramatically, and there was no denying that some of those changes were quite uncomfortable. She had gone from a penniless companion dependent upon a difficult employer for her very existence, to one of the most sought-after heiresses in England literally overnight, and there were times when she wondered if she might have imagined it all.

In a single afternoon she had received more proposals than she had had in the whole of her life, until she was forced to take refuge with Mr. Bigley, her late great-uncle's solicitor, and his wife. It had been he who hired Constance, insisting she needed a companion to lend her consequence, and it was on his advice that she was now journeying to her fammily's estate of Bridge's Leap, located on the Cornish coast.

She'd only been teasing Constance when she mentioned the possibility of a plot against her, but now her mind was filled with doubts. What if the accidents plaguing her were no accident? What if she had an enemy who wished her dead? What if . . . She shook her head, feeling faintly embarrassed by the gothic turn her imagination had taken.

"No, Constance," she said, her small chin coming up with determination, "of course I don't. You are right, and those accidents were mostly my doing. Although—" her eyes took on a twinkle "—if one more untoward thing does happen, I may take to wondering if I have insulted a gypsy or some such thing! Now, come and let us unpack our things. Dinner is less than three hours away, and I want to make a proper appearance. If I am to be mistress of Bride's Leap, 'tis time I began acting the part.''

"What do you mean you wish to rent out the parlor?" Sir Ian Charles demanded, his sea blue eyes narrowing with fury. "You have already rented out the parlor to me, and I'll be damned if I'll share it with anyone!"

"But, Cap'n, these be ladies!" Mr. Pruitt wailed, wringing his hands as he saw his bonus from Miss Chambers slipping from his grasp. "I can't let 'em sup in my taproom; it wouldn't be proper!"

"Then let them eat in their own rooms!" Ian growled, furious by the innkeeper's inopportunities. He had ridden out from Marchfield earlier that day with Jacinda's angry warnings ringing in his ears. The ride had aggravated his wound, and he'd arrived feeling decidedly the worse for wear. He hired the parlor at once, anticipating a solitary evening spent drinking until he could no longer feel the burning pain in his shoulder, and by God, that is precisely what he would do.

"The lady, Miss Chambers she be called, said as how she misliked dinin' in her room," Mr. Pruitt continued, still hopeful that he might convince the cold-eyed man standing in front of him to see the sweet light of reason. "I'm sure if you was to ask, she'd be more than willing to pay you for—"

"I am not a cit to be turned out of my room merely because someone has greased your palm with a half crown!" Ian thundered, temporarily forgetting the role he had assumed for his journey to Cornwall. "If this blasted female must have a private room to

12

be satisfied, it has nothing to do with me. The room is mine."

The innkeeper licked his thick lips, searching for some way to solve his dilemma. He disliked the notion of disappointing Miss Chambers and her fat purse, but he was equally unwilling to cross the captain. The man had the hard look of danger about him, and he knew it would be foolhardy to press him too far. Then he remembered the cask of French brandy hidden in his storeroom. Nothing like a drop of brandy to make a gentleman agreeable, he reasoned, brightening with hope.

"As you say, Cap'n," he said in a hearty manner that made Ian's dark gold eyebrows meet in a suspicious scowl. "I s'pose if Miss Chambers and her companion be hungry enough, they'll eat in their rooms and like it. I'll tell her the room ain't to be had. In the meanwhile, I'll have the boy fetch you up some brandy. It be a bit chilly tonight, eh?" He winked jovially.

Ian grunted, and satisfied with his response, Mr. Pruitt drifted away, closing the door to Ian's bedchamber behind him. Once he was alone, Ian loosened his cravat with an impatient tug, flinging himself in the worn burgundy velvet chair that stood before the fireplace.

Perhaps he should have agreed to letting the blasted female share his room, he brooded, swinging a booted foot idly. It was what any gentleman would do; especially a half-pay captain newly cashiered from His Majesty's service. Such a man, he reasoned, would be falling all over himself to oblige a lady well heeled enough to have a grasping thief like Pruitt so eager to do her bidding. That he had failed to do so was certain to arouse the innkeeper's suspicions, and as he was forever telling his agents, when it came to assuming a disguise, no detail was too small to ignore.

He had just about decided to ring for Pruitt to inform him of his change of heart when there was a knock on the door and a footman entered, a tray bearing a decanter and a glass held precariously in his hands. "Here's your brandy, Captain," he said, placing the tray on the chest at the foot of Ian's bed. "Mr. Pruitt said you was to help yourself; no charge."

Ian's suspicions were instantly aroused. Pruitt struck him as the sort who would charge his own starving mother for a crust of bread. His eyes flicked towards the dark amber liquid in the decanter. "French brandy?" he asked, making no move to pour the wine.

"Mr. Pruitt buys only the best," the footman declared, pouring a generous portion of brandy and offering it to Ian. "Here's to your health, sir."

Ian stared at the glass, and for a moment he was back on that fog-shrouded beach in France, watching in helpless rage as his men were gunned down by smugglers armed with rifles they had traded for brandy. His lips thinned coldly. "I don't drink French brandy," he said, his voice dangerously soft. "Take it away."

"But Mr. Pruitt said—"

He was on his feet in a flash, his right hand lashing out and sending the glass flying from the startled footman's hand. "Mr. Pruitt may go to the devil!" he snarled, towering over the footman. "I won't touch a drop of his damned brandy; now, get out of here. Wait," he added as the younger man rushed to do his bidding.

"Y-yes, sir?" The footman cast him a frightened look over his shoulder.

"You may tell Mr. Pruitt I have reconsidered, and that I should be delighted to share my room with Miss Chambers and her companion," Ian said, making a determined effort to regain control of his temper.

"Yes sir, Captain Sherrill," the footman answered with obvious relief. He turned towards the door as Ian called out to him.

"What is your name?"

"Dicks, Captain."

Ian dug into the pocket of his green and silver waistcoat, extracting a coin, which he flipped to the footman. "This is for your trouble, Dicks," he said, smiling as the lad pocketed the money. "Thank you."

"You're welcome, Captain." But rather than hurrying away, he stood by the door, shifting uncertainly from one foot to the other.

Ian gave a weary sigh. "What is it, Dicks?"

"Well, there be a minister and his sister stayin' here," the footman explained, his words tripping over themselves in their eagerness to get out. "Mr. Pruitt says as how having a gentleman of the cloth in the taproom be bad for business, and he was thinking—"

"No, absolutely not," Ian said decisively, deciding there were limits even to a half-pay captain's patience. "I don't mind sharing my parlor with two ladies, but I draw the line at members of the clergy. Is that clear?"

Dicks broke into a wide grin. "Aye, that it does, sir. Thank ye for being so kind."

"You're most welcome, Dicks," Ian replied, giving him one of his rare smiles. "I only hope that Miss Chambers and her companion aren't inveterate gabblers; although I suppose that would be too much to wish for. They are female, after all."

Maggie stood in front of her tiered glass, turning first this way and then that as she studied her reflection. The green silk gown with its heart-shaped bodice and fashionably dropped waist showed her tall and slender form to its best advantage, and was a definite improvement over the dowdy gowns she had worn as a companion. Even her hair was arranged differently; the fiery curls with their gold highlights bound in an elegant chignon, rather than pinned back in the stern coronet of braids Mrs. Graft had deemed a suitable coiffure. Small diamonds flashed at her ears, and for the first time in her life, she felt almost pretty.

No, she amended with a self-deprecatory smile, not pretty; at five and twenty, she considered herself far too old for that particular sobriquet. But she did feel lovely, and buoyed with a new sense of confidence, she turned to retrieve her reticule from the stool. She had just picked it up when Constance entered the room, her face lighting up at the sight of her employer.

"Why, Miss Chambers, how beautiful you look!" she cried, her blue eyes bright with approval as she studied Maggie's careful toilet. "Captain Sherrill is certain to fall at your feet the moment he claps eyes on you!"

Maggie's pleasure with her appearance faded at Constance's light bantering. Since inheriting the money, she had become overly sensitive to the very suggestion that she was attempting to fix a man's interest, and she shot the other woman an indignant scowl. "Really, Constance, as if I should dress to attract a man I have never met!" she snapped, her voice unconsciously harsh. "I dress to suit myself, and I don't give a fig if the captain likes it or not!"

Constance's smile wavered and then collapsed under the weight of Maggie's glare. "I am very sorry, Miss Chambers," she said, bending her blond head over her clasped hands. "I meant no insult. I-I was only teasing you."

Maggie was instantly contrite. Many times in the not-so-distant past, she had been made to suffer for the vagaries of her employer's temper, and she had always vowed never to treat her servants in a similar fashion. That she had done so appalled her, and she was eager to make amends. "No, it is I who should apologize," she said, giving Constance a penitent smile. "I had no right to snap at you like that. Pray accept my apologies and allow me to compliment you on your appearance. You are looking fine as a sixpence."

"Thank you, Miss Chambers." Constance stroked the sheer blue and silver skirts of her stylish gown. "It's one of the new ones you were kind enough to purchase for me. Do you like it?"

"It's quite beautiful," Maggie approved, grateful that the awkward moment had passed. And truth to tell, she did admire the other woman's dress. Like most tall women, she adored dainty, frilly things, and Constance's gown, with its silver net overskirt and puffy sleeves, was so delicately crafted, it might have been worn by Titania.

Poor Constance. Maggie's eyes rested on the blonde's head with a sudden surge of affection; what a dreadful life she had led this past year. She spoke little of herself or her past, but Maggie had learned from Mr. Bigley that the poor child had lost her whole family to the fever, and was now cast penniless into the world. Having been in that very same position less than eight years ago, she could easily identify with the other girl's plight, and she was glad that she was able to offer her a position now.

As they made their way downstairs, Maggie kept glancing at her beautiful companion. Perhaps it was just as well that she had no intention of setting her cap at the captain, she thought with a rueful smile. It was unlikely any man would pay her any attention once he had clapped eyes on Constance. Not that she was desirous of any such attention, she told herself primly, but still, a small flirtation never hurt anyone. It might even prove instructive.

She knew her experience in dealing with the male sex was limited, at best, and if the past few weeks were any indication, it was a skill she would be wise to acquire. How else was she to learn how to handle fortune hunters and the like unless she obtained some experience? She didn't think the captain to be such a man, but surely it wouldn't hurt if she honed her meager skills on him?

Yes, she decided, her heart beginning to pound with anticipation. That is precisely what she would do. She would smile at the captain and play the coquette until she determined the stripe of man he was. If she succeeded in fixing his interest, fine, and if not, she would still have gained valuable experience. He need never be the wiser, and after tomorrow, it was doubtful she would ever see him again. How could she possibly lose?

Chapter Two

Jan stood with his back to the fireplace, a glass cradled in his hand, as he waited for the ladies to join him. He had spent the intervening two hours resting and preparing for this meeting. He had subtly interviewed the servants, learning as much as he could about the lady with whom he would soon be sharing his parlor, and what he learned intrigued him.

Miss Chambers was said to be quite rich; an heiress who had recently come into an unexpected inheritance. She was also reputed to be quite lovely, although he put this down to her generosity with the staff. Even the plainest of women would be counted upon as handsome if her pockets were deep enough, and Miss Chambers's pockets were evidently quite deep indeed. He had no quarrel with her wealth, although it did rankle him that she was using it to try and oust him from his parlor.

He was also curious about where she had obtained her alleged fortune. He made it a point to be kept au courant with the *ton*, and yet her name was completely unknown to him. The possibility that she was an adventuress posing as an heiress had already occurred to him, and he decided it might be interesting to play her along. If nothing else, it would help while away an otherwise dull evening, and God knew he had enough of those before him as it was.

The thought of his forced inactivity brought a flash of anger to his eyes. He knew the prince meant well, but a holiday was the last thing he needed now. He had spent the past ten years of his life in the clandestine world of espionage, and it was all he knew. Cut off as he was from all that was familiar left him feeling lost and alone; sensations that frankly troubled him. If he was this maudlin after a mere twenty-four hours away from his post, what the devil would he be like at the end of a month?

Thankfully the door to the parlor opened and Dicks stepped inside, two ladies trailing at his heels. "Miss Chambers and Miss Spenser, Captain Marcus Sherrill," he said, executing a credible bow.

"Thank you, Dicks." Ian's eyes flashed to the tall redhead with the stormy gray eyes, whom he recognized from the servants' description. She wasn't beautiful in the conventional sense of the word, not with that imperious nose and stubborn chin, but he found her soft mouth and expressive eyes rather intriguing. Dismissing her after that one glance, he turned to Dicks, his manner coolly impeccable as he said, "Please inform the cook that we will be ready to eat within the hour. If that is acceptable to you, Miss Chambers?" His tone was faintly challenging as he gave her a polite smile. The pretty redhead might dress the lady, but he knew a hoyden when he saw one, and thought it best to establish his mastery of the situation from the start.

"That will be fine, Captain Sherrill, thank you," Maggie replied, her guard coming up at the captain's tone. Heavens, what a haughty fellow he was, she thought, striving to hide her displeasure from his watchful blue eyes. Had she not wished to give the appearance of being thoroughly routed, she would have turned and stalked out of the parlor then and there. Even dining in her tiny room was preferable to putting up with the captain's patent hostility.

After Dicks departed, Ian did the pretty by offering both ladies sherry, and they settled on the chairs arranged in front of the fireplace. While Constance and the captain engaged in polite conversation, Maggie sipped her sherry, studying him through her lashes. It was a pity he was so priggish, she mused, a tiny smile of devilry touching her mouth, for he really was quite handsome. He was tall, six feet at least, and she was willing to hazard that his broad shoulders owed little to the buckram padding most dandies used in their jackets. His dark gold hair was worn longer than was the fashion, and it was swept back from his broad forehead with a casual yet masculine grace. His aristocratic nose and high cheekbones gave his face character, and yet it was his eyes that caught and held her attention. They were the color of a summer sea, changing from blue to green with the flickering firelight, and she found herself wondering about the lack of warmth in their shimmering depths.

There was a sudden silence in the room, and Maggie became aware the other two were staring at her with obvious confusion. She felt a warm blush steal across her face at having been caught gaping at the captain like a love-struck moon calf, and she fastened a cool smile on her lips.

"Might I ask what regiment you are with, Captain?" she said, hiding her embarrassment with admirable calm. "I notice you aren't in uniform. Are you on leave, perhaps?"

"I was most recently posted in America, Miss Chambers," Ian answered, slipping easily into the role he had invented. "But with the cessation of hostilities, I find myself without a command, so it's back to Cornwall for me. Where are you ladies making for, if I may be so bold? Paris? All the world is gone there, or so I have heard."

"The world may go where it will, but as for Constance and me, we are also bound for Cornwall," Maggie replied, mollified by the captain's response. Perhaps she had been too hasty in her judgment of him, she decided.

"Indeed?" Ian's eyebrows arched at the news. "How intriguing. Where in Cornwall are you going?"

"The nearest village is Mevagissey, but the house itself is known as Bride's Leap," Maggie provided, eager to put the earlier unpleasantness behind them. "Perhaps you have heard of it?"

"Ah yes," he answered vaguely, for the house did have a familiar ring to it. "Is it as lovely as they say?" he asked, hoping she would say something that would trigger his memory.

"Actually, I've never seen it," Maggie confessed with a candid smile. "I've just inherited it, and this will be my first visit there. Although I must say I am looking forward to the experience; it's said to be haunted, you know." Her eyes sparkled with laughter.

Ian blinked in surprise. Good lord, the whole thing sounded like something out of a Minervian novel, he thought, his mouth twisting derisively. An unexpected inheritance, a haunted mansion; the plot needed only a murderous villain and a hidden treasure to be complete.

"At least, that is what Mr. Bigley, Great-Uncle

22

Ellsworth's solicitor, told me." Maggie determinedly ignored her host's cool expression. "He seemed terribly afraid I would refuse the inheritance and then he would have to spend even more time locating another heir."

In a flash Ian knew why he had recognized the name of her country house. "Good lord, Bride's Leap!" he exclaimed, staring down at her in surprise. "*You're* Ellsworth Simington's long-lost heir?"

He remembered the story now; it had been in all the London papers some months ago. An elderly recluse had died after a long illness, leaving a fortune of some one hundred thousand pounds to his "nearest living relation," and the search for the lucky heir was on. The search had captured the public's attention until Napoleon's abdication had pushed it to the back pages of some of the minor gazettes. He'd completely forgotten about the story until just this moment.

Talking of her inheritance always made Maggie feel uneasy, for she had never felt entitled to the staggering sum. "Yes, I am," she admitted, hiding her sudden uneasiness behind bright chatter. "Did you know him? We never met, and all I knew of him is what my grandfather had told my mother, and that, I fear, was far from complimentary. Considering that the family was estranged for almost fifty years, I never expected to get so much as a farthing, let alone the entire one hundred thousand pounds."

Ian shook his head at her frank confession. He had spent a great deal of his adult life guarding his every word, his every expression, and he found it inconceivable that she could sit there and blithely tell a complete stranger the personal details of her life. His dark gold eyebrows slammed together in an angry scowl.

"If I were you, Miss Chambers, I would be a little less free with such information," he informed her in the cutting tones of a superior dressing down a junior officer. "These are desperate times, and kidnappings are not unheard-of. It might be advisable for you to avoid flaunting your good fortune until you are safely home."

Maggie's uneasiness vanished in a flare of temper at his words and the condescending manner in which he had spoken them. Of all the arrogant, overbearing beasts, she fumed, her gray eyes flashing with defiance. She had been right about him from the very start; the man was toplofty beyond all endurance.

"I beg your pardon, Captain Sherrill," she said, her pointed chin coming up as she met him glare for glare. "But I don't believe I was 'flaunting' my good fortune, as you call it. You asked if I was Uncle Ellsworth's heir, and I confirmed it. Not," she added with a haughty sniff, "that I consider the matter to be any of your business."

"Miss Chambers!" Constance was clearly scandalized by her employer's rude behavior. "Captain Sherrill was but making an observation, and he does have the right of it, you know. You should be more cautious."

"Nonsense," Maggie grumbled, annoyed by what she considered to be Constance's defection. "The pair of you act as if I go about with a placard that says 'Heiress Available' about my neck. I shouldn't have said a word about it if he hadn't mentioned it first."

"Are you at least traveling with a groom or some sort of male guardian to lend you protection?" Ian demanded, ignoring her sarcasm. He couldn't believe any female could be so hen-witted as to travel unescorted in these dangerous times, although he strongly suspected that was precisely what the little minx was doing. She struck him as the type who would do whatever she damned well pleased.

"I am five and twenty, Captain, and I require neither groom nor guardian to guide me from Exeter to Cornwall," Maggie informed him in a voice that dripped with icy fury. After spending the last eight years of her life mutinously following her employer's selfish commands, she had promised herself that she would never be dictated to again. And certainly not by an insufferably arrogant stranger met by chance in a country inn.

"Then how do you intend to get to Cornwall?" Ian asked, although he suspected he already knew the answer.

"Why, by mail coach, Captain." Maggie sent him a falsely sweet smile. "How will *you* be traveling?"

"I am also traveling by mail coach," he returned stiffly, shooting her a look that had been known to make even brave men step back a pace.

"What? Without a groom or guardian to lend you protection?" she asked, fluttering her lashes at him coquettishly. "For shame, sir, have you no care for your reputation?"

"Well, I for one shall welcome your presence, Captain," Constance said, sending Maggie a gentle frown of disapproval. "We had originally planned to travel by private coach, but there was some sort of difficulty. I am sure we shall all have a lovely journey together."

The arrival of dinner gave Ian the opportunity to regain control of himself. He had always taken pride in his ability to command his emotions regardless of the situation, and he couldn't like his response to the argumentative Miss Chambers. Evidently his injury was causing him more discomfort than he realized, he thought, stoically hiding a grimace of pain as he held out Miss Spenser's chair for her.

Maggie spent the first part of the meal concentrating on her stringy, overcooked beef and silently admonishing herself for her petulant behavior. Now that her temper had cooled, she knew Captain Sherrill meant her no personal insult, and that it was probably just his nature to be so commanding.

"Where were you posted in America, Captain?" Constance asked, smiling at Ian as they lingered over their food. "I had a dear friend, William Clayburt, who was assigned to our regiment at Baltimore, and I was wondering if perhaps you knew him?"

"Unfortunately not, Miss Spenser. I was with one of our outposts in the Carolinas, and I fear we had little contact with the other garrisons," Ian replied, keeping his answers deliberately vague. He also made a note of Clayburt's name, more out of habit than necessity. In his business, it was never wise to overlook even the smallest detail.

"I have heard that the Americans keep slaves in the Carolinas," Maggie said, deciding she had been silent long enough. "Is that so?"

"There were several large plantations in the area around Charleston that kept slaves," Ian admitted cautiously, not quite trusting Miss Chambers's polite smile. "But as we were too busy fighting to stay alive, I am afraid there was little we could do to remedy the situation."

Maggie blinked at his grim tone. "I did not mean to imply that you should," she said, noting the pinched look about his mouth and the hard glitter in his eyes. Then she recalled the stiff way he had bowed when they had been introduced, and the look of pain on his face when he helped Constance into her chair.

"Is that where you were wounded?" she asked, realizing the reasons behind his earlier ill humor.

26

The poor man was doubtlessly in a great deal of pain.

Ian glared at her. He had hoped to keep his infirmity a secret, and he was furious at her acuity. " 'Tis nothing," he said, his tone curt. "A farewell present from an American marksman, that is all. You must not trouble yourself."

"But it is obviously troubling you," Maggie protested, her brows gathering in a worried frown. "Perhaps it is infected, and you should have it examined by a physician. I am sure Mr. Pruitt could send for one and—"

"No!" Ian snapped, then aware he was being rude, he added, "The sawbones on the ship warned me my arm would be stiff for several months to come, and advised me to take care. I fear I must have overestimated my strength." And he forced himself to give her a cool smile.

"But a wound that is still plaguing you months later can't be good," Maggie insisted, her lips firming with determination. "You must have it examined by a doctor. I insist."

Ian's cup clattered in its saucer as he set it down, but before he could speak, the door to the parlor was flung open and a small woman dressed in black serge came sailing into the room, a tall man in the somber garb of the clergy trailing at her heels.

"I am Miss Leonora Thomas," she announced in a loud voice, "and this is my brother, the Reverend Robert Thomas; you may call him Brother Thomas. Our apologies for being late, but that fool of a footman would insist that you had refused to share your parlor with a man of God. Naturally I informed him he was mistaken." And she took a chair at the table.

Ian stared down at her, temporarily rendered speechless by her sheer gall. His eyes moved from her plain features to Miss Chambers's face, and all hostility between them vanished as they exchanged identical looks of disbelief. The disbelief slowly gave way to amusement, but when he turned to Miss Thomas, there was no evidence of humor in his gaze.

"I am afraid it is *you* who are mistaken," he said, his voice as cold and cutting as a blade. "Dicks was but repeating my instructions. This is a private parlor, and I will thank you and your brother to leave it." His eyes flicked towards Brother Robert, who had already discovered the sherry decanter and was helping himself to the contents.

Instead of taking umbrage at what was the cut direct, Miss Thomas folded her hands primly in front of her, beaming up at Ian in delight. "As soldiers of the Lord, my brother and I are used to ill treatment at the hands of sinners," she informed them with obvious pride. "Nonetheless, we shall stand firm in our duty and pray that by our example, we bring you back to the paths of light." Her jet-colored eyes moved over Maggie and Constance with mercenary intent. "Which of you is the heiress everyone is gossiping about?"

Maggie bit her lip to hold back a laugh. Really, the woman was not to be believed. Evidently Captain Sherrill was right, and it would have been wiser not to flaunt her newfound wealth, although she knew she would die sooner than admit as much.

"I am Miss Chambers," she said, unconsciously mimicking Mrs. Graft at her imperious best. "May I ask what possible business it might be of yours?"

"My brother and I are always happy to accept donations from pious folk anxious to help us in our work," came the swift reply as Miss Thomas leaned forward with an eager smile.

"How interesting," Maggie smiled coolly, "and should I encounter any pious folk, I shall be certain to tell them. Now, if you will excuse my companion and me, it has been rather a long day." She rose to her feet and offered her hand to Ian.

"Captain, my thanks again for sharing your parlor with us. It was most kind of you."

"You're welcome, Miss Chambers," Ian murmured, admiration and not a small amount of amusement sparkling in his eyes as he accepted her hand. "But pray allow me to escort you and Miss Spenser to the stairs; heaven only knows what sort of riffraff might be waiting outside the door."

A loud sniff from Miss Thomas's direction let Ian know his insult had not gone unnoticed, and he excused himself curtly as he led them from the room. After thanking the captain, Constance bade them both good night, and slipped quietly up the stairs. Once they were alone, Maggie turned to Ian.

"Riffraff?" she repeated, her gray eyes dancing as she gazed up at him. "Isn't that doing it a shade too brown?"

"Not at all. The only difference between a cutpurse and Miss Thomas is that the cutpurse makes no secret about what he is," Ian argued smoothly. "And you are a fine one to talk. What of the shameful way you are abandoning me to those two? Is that any way to treat a wounded soldier?"

"I have every faith in your powers of perseverance," Maggie assured him with a soft laugh. "Besides, there's no reason for you to return to the parlor, is there? They have what they want; leave them to it."

"A good soldier never abandons the field to the enemy," Ian told her with feigned indignation. "It is a matter of principle that I return and drive them out. I only hope she doesn't come up to your rooms and plague you. She strikes me as the kind of woman who would stop at nothing."

"If she does, you may be very sure I shan't hesitate to call for assistance," Maggie laughed, ex-

tending her hand to him. "Good night, Captain
Sherrill, and may I wish you well routing the enemy? Although I have no doubt but that you will
emerge victorious."

"Thank you, Miss Chambers," Ian murmured,
carrying her hand to his lips for a brief kiss. "God-
speed and a pleasant journey to both you and Miss
Spenser."

After he had departed, Maggie turned and made
her way up the stairs. The sounds of laughter and
merrymaking came from the taproom, and Maggie
was grateful she and Constance had taken rooms
far from the other travelers, otherwise she doubted
they would get any sleep.

The price of her rooms also provided her with the
services of a maid, but as it was late, she decided
against summoning her. She still wasn't accustomed to the luxury of servants, and there were
some things she preferred to do for herself. A half
smile touched her lips as she closed the door behind
her, tossing her reticule on the dressing table.

The small rush of air directly behind her was her
only warning as a shrouded figure stepped from the
shadows to grab her. She opened her lips, but the
scream she would have uttered was muffled by
the hard hand that clamped over her mouth. Maggie fought frantically, but she was no match for her
assailant as he began dragging her across the room.

Her first thought was that he meant to rob her,
but when she saw the bed, another more dreadful
possibility occurred to her. She renewed her strug-
gles, and managed to pull free of his suffocating
grasp. The moment her mouth was free, she threw
back her head and screamed, praying that she could
be heard above the din from below. She ran for the
door, but even as her fingers closed about the handle, her attacker was on her again.

A gloved hand slammed into the side of her head,

stunning her. She felt the man shifting her over his arm, and realized somewhat dazedly that he was dragging her out into the hall. Her consciousness began to fade. She could feel the toes of her slippers dragging on the carpet and tried to gain purchase by digging them in, slowing her assailant down, if only temporarily.

There was a sudden shout and the thud of approaching footsteps, and then she was dropped somewhat roughly to the floor as the man holding her turned to face her rescuer. She could hear the battle being fought above her, and struggled for breath for another scream. The sound of flesh striking flesh was followed by a harsh intake of air and a vicious oath, and the echo of retreating footsteps as someone—her attacker, she prayed—fled down the hall.

She lay in a crumpled heap at the top of the stairs, vaguely aware of shouts and cries of alarm. Then someone was turning her gently over, murmuring soft reassurances to her. It was only then that she realized her eyes were closed, and she fought to open them. The hallway was dark, but not so dark that she didn't recognize the grim-faced man bending over her.

"Captain Sherrill," she gasped, staring up into his sea-colored eyes, "what are you doing here?" And then, to her everlasting shame, she collapsed into a dead faint.

Chapter Three

Jan was halfway to the parlor when he became aware of a cold prickling between his shoulder blades. He stopped, his head tilted to one side as he concentrated on the sensation of danger that increased with each passing second. He had experienced this phenomenon only twice before; the last time being less than a week ago when he had been scrambling down a beach path, wondering if he could trust the man in front of him. Without pausing to question his instincts, he turned and started towards the staircase, certain the threat came from somewhere up there. He'd only taken a few steps when he heard the muffled scream.

He dashed up the remaining stairs; rounding the corner just as a door at the end of the darkened passage flew open and a man dragging a struggling woman came backing out. It took him less than a second to recognize Miss Chambers and then he was stepping forward, the knife he had pulled from his sleeve held at the ready.

"You there, stop!"

The man swung around, his eyes glittering behind the black mask he wore over his head. He froze as if startled by Ian's presence, and then he began dragging Miss Chambers backwards, his intentions all too obvious to Ian. The bastard was going to throw her down the staircase! With a harsh cry, he launched himself forward, determined to wrest her from her attacker's grasp.

As he anticipated, the man dropped Miss Chambers to the floor, and then turned to meet his rush. Even handicapped as he was, Ian managed to land the first blow, the sharp blade of his knife slashing through the man's black cloak. The man countered with a hard punch to Ian's bad shoulder, sending a burning pain down his arm. Still he fought on, ignoring the agony that made his senses swim.

He managed to knock his opponent backwards and away from Miss Chambers, but even as he followed to administer another blow, he heard a shout from down the hall as two men came racing towards them. The other man regained his balance and then turned to flee down the backstairs, disappearing into the darkness. Ian followed, but by the time he reached the bottom of the stairs, the man was nowhere to be seen.

Blast it all, but he must be getting old, Ian thought, rubbing his shoulder as he made his way to where a crowd was already gathering over Miss Chambers; a year ago and the whoreson would never have made it past him. He pushed his way through the gawking crowd, his sensitive fingers feeling for a pulse as he knelt beside her. It was only as he felt the life pumping through her that he began to relax. Until this moment, he hadn't allowed himself to hope she was unharmed.

At his touch, her thick lashes fluttered and then opened, and a pair of hazy gray eyes regarded him with confusion. "Captain Sherrill," she whispered, her voice soft and somewhat slurred, "what are you

33

doing here?" And then she collapsed in his strong arms.

" 'Ere, what's this?" Ian heard the landlord's blustering voice as he elbowed his way forward. At the sight of Ian holding the unconscious woman in his arms, he skittered to a halt. "What the bloody hell—"

"Miss Chambers has been attacked," Ian snapped, his cold voice cutting into Mr. Pruitt's horrified protestations. "I chased the bastard off, but there's a chance he might still be lurking about. He's approximately six feet tall, and was wearing dark clothing and a dark mask. I would check the stables and the other rooms if I were you; God only knows where he may be hiding or what he may have already taken."

This sent most of the crowd scurrying to their rooms to check their belongings, leaving Ian alone save for the innkeeper. Not trusting the heavyset man with his precious burden, he scooped Miss Chambers up in his arms and carried her into what he assumed was her room. He had no sooner placed her on the bed than he began rapping out orders.

"Check your register to see if you have a physician staying here," he instructed, brushing back a strand of bright red hair that had fallen across Miss Chambers's pale cheek. "If so, bring him at once; if not, fetch one."

"Now, see here, Captain Sherrill, I'll thank ye to—"

"And then send for that companion of hers." Ian ignored his indignant protest. "I'll not have Miss Chambers tended to by one of your tavern wenches."

"But—"

"Do it now."

The deadly threat in Ian's softly spoken words, as well as the cold glitter in his eyes, sent Mr.

Pruitt stumbling for the door. Ian turned his attention back to Miss Chambers, noting with relief that her cheeks had regained some of their color. Even as he watched, her soft lips parted in a gasp and her eyes blinked open. She stared up at Ian, her brows gathering in a puzzled frown.

"I didn't faint," she announced, her voice decisive for all its weakness. "I have never fainted in all my life."

"I am sure you have not," Ian replied, amused by her evident embarrassment. "But then, I'll wager you've never been attacked, either."

"I'm not so sure of that," she muttered, rubbing her temples and frowning up at him as if she held him responsible for her discomfort. "Well, did you at least catch the scoundrel? I think he meant to rob me!"

Ian frowned at her question. Any other female of his acquaintance would be having a strong case of the vapors by now, and her rather cavalier acceptance of the situation puzzled him. Had she been expecting something like this? he wondered, studying her with suspicion.

"Judging from the careless way you announced your inheritance to one and all, I shouldn't be surprised," he said, his anger stirring now that he knew she was safe. "Did I not warn you that such candidness might prove dangerous?"

Maggie's jaw dropped. "Do you mean to say that you blame this ... this assault on *me*?" she demanded, propping herself up on one elbow as she glared at him. The impropriety of their situation had occurred to her, but she brushed it aside impatiently, too angry to bother with such fustian as false modesty. Her fear turned outward in an indignant fury, and had she possessed the strength, she would have slapped the arrogant look from his handsome face.

"Just who the devil do you think you are?" she demanded, her volatile emotions erupting in a blaze of temper. "I might have been killed . . . or worse, and all you can tell me is that I am somehow to blame? How dare you!"

"I dare because it is true," Ian retorted with a considerable degree of heat. His shoulder was throbbing like the very devil, and his customary control was quite beyond him. When he thought about what might have happened to Miss Chambers had he not acted on his instincts, he felt like smashing something. But rather than thanking him for his efforts, the little minx was actually scolding him, her gray eyes spitting fire like a cat's.

"Why, you puffed-up, overbearing—"

"Miss Chambers! Miss Chambers! Are you all right?" Constance came dashing into the room, her blond hair flowing down her back. "Oh my heavens, what has happened?" She pushed her way past Ian and collapsed at her employer's bedside. "Mr. Pruitt said you were attacked!"

"I am fine, Constance," Maggie replied, making a heroic effort to master her errant emotions. "There was a man waiting in my rooms, and when I stepped inside, he grabbed me."

Constance paled, her face turning the same shade as the white dressing gown that draped her slender body. "He . . . he did not . . ." She placed a hand over her throat, her blue eyes eloquent as she silently asked the question she dared not voice aloud.

"No," Maggie assured her gruffly, embarrassed color staining her cheeks. "He dragged me out into the hall, and apparently Captain Sherrill was able to fight him off. I was just thanking him for his kindness when you came in." And she gave him a tight smile, daring him to dispute her explanation.

"Thank you, dearest, dearest sir!" Constance cried, turning tear-filled blue eyes in Ian's direction. "Mr. Pruitt told me how you single-handedly defeated the villain and then carried Miss Chambers to her rooms, and I shall be eternally in your debt! I do not know what I should have done had anything happened to her!"

Mr. Pruitt returned at that moment, a sleepy-eyed guest in tow whom Ian took for the doctor. The plump man with his pale hair and cherubic face looked rather young to be a doctor, but there was no faulting his professionalism as he bent over Miss Chambers's bed.

"I am Dr. Adam Burke; our innkeeper informs me you've had something of a shock," he said, taking Maggie's hand in his. "I understand you were unconscious for some while?"

"I fainted," Maggie admitted gruffly, still feeling faintly ashamed of her missish behavior. She flicked her eyes in Captain Sherrill's direction, noting somewhat petulantly that he was leaning against the door with his arms folded across his chest. A gentleman would have departed by now out of respect for her privacy, but apparently the captain had no intention of leaving her side.

"Of course you did," the doctor soothed, flashing her a reassuring smile as he checked her pulse. "The whole experience must have been quite horrifying for you. Now, with your permission, I should like to examine you ... with your companion in attendance, of course." He acknowledged Constance with an inclination of his head.

Ian decided it was time for him to slip quietly away. Now that Miss Chambers was more or less in capable hands, he was free to do some discreet snooping. There were several questions that plagued him, and he knew he'd never find the answers hanging about here. His mind made up, he began inching his way out the door.

Maggie caught the captain's furtive movement

out of the corner of her eye, and her brows puckered in a troubled frown. Despite her annoyance with his high-handed ways, she was still grateful for his assistance, and she realized with a guilty flush that she hadn't so much as thanked him. Then she remembered Constance had said something about him carrying her, and she called out, "Captain Sherrill, wait!"

"Yes, Miss Chambers?" Ian cast her a wary glance.

"I . . . how is your shoulder?" she asked, nervously moistening her lips with the tip of her tongue. "You didn't reinjure it when you carried me, did you?"

"Not at all," he lied, wondering if the chit was part witch. His whole arm ached almost as much as it had after he'd been shot, and he prayed he hadn't torn open the wound.

Maggie hesitated. His response was anything but encouraging, but she wasn't about to stop now. "Perhaps you might have Dr. Burke look at it," she pressed with dogged determination. "Before dinner you mentioned it has been plaguing you, and I am sure the good doctor wouldn't mind."

Ian hid his annoyance behind a carefully blank expression. Miss Chambers was without doubt the most obstinate female he had ever encountered, and he was torn between fury and admiration. It had been years since anyone had challenged his authority as consistently as had she.

"Perhaps later," he prevaricated, not wishing to debate the issue in front of the others. He had already drawn enough attention to himself, and he wanted only to slip quitely away so that he could begin his investigation.

Maggie regarded him suspiciously, realizing, much to her disgust, that there was nothing she could do. She could hardly insist that the doctor examine him against his will. "Very well, Captain," she said, her chin coming up as she regarded him with cool dignity. "Pray accept my thanks for your courage and quick thinking. I shudder to think what might have happened had it not been for you."

"You're most welcome, Miss Chambers," Ian replied with a polite bow. He could only guess at how much it must have galled her to swallow her monumental pride, and he felt a grudging respect for her courage. The thought of someone attempting to harm her was a sudden anathema to him, and he was filled with a deadly resolve to catch the person or persons responsible.

"Yes, thank you once again, Captain Sherrill." Constance had risen to her feet and drifted over to stand in front of Ian, her head tilted back as she gave him a dazzling smile. "We shall never forget what you have done, will we, Miss Chambers?"

"Indeed we shall not, Constance," Maggie replied, her eyes meeting the captain's in a look of mutual understanding. "In fact, I think it safe to say that the captain's memory shall be with me for a very long time."

Ian's lips quirked in an appreciative smile. He might have known the vixen was a long way from being vanquished. "As shall yours with me, Miss Chambers. As shall yours with me."

Ian spent the next two hours searching the area and discreetly questioning the guests and staff. A quick check of the other rooms revealed none of them had been so much as entered, and no one could recall seeing or hearing anything out of the ordinary. Disgusted by his lack of progress, he finally gave up and retired to his rooms for the evening, his expression deeply troubled.

After donning his nightclothes, he climbed into bed, folding his arms beneath his head as he stared up at the ceiling. The action pulled on his stitches, but he ignored the pain, concentrating instead on the evening's events. What the devil was going on?

He was a trained spy, his years of experience giving him abilities other men could only guess at, and yet he'd found no sign of the masked intruder. The man was a professional, obviously, but a professional what? Certainly not a thief, for he had seen Miss Chambers's reticule lying on the top of her dresser. And if his intent had been to rape her, then why had he dragged her out into the hallway, where his chances of being caught were greatly increased? It made no sense.

The only thing he did know was that he could not let Miss Chambers journey any further on her own. It was obvious she was in danger, and he wasn't the sort of man who could turn his back on anyone in need . . . even a recalcitrant little hoyden with a temper that matched her fiery hair. Since no one was expecting him, there was no earthly reason why he couldn't escort her and Miss Spenser to Bride's Leap. It was the gentlemanly sort of thing to do, he assured himself, and on the way there, he could interrogate them at his leisure.

Yes, he decided, a pleased smile touching his lips, that is precisely what he would do. He would accompany the ladies on their journey, and by the time they reached Mevagissey, he would have the answers to the questions that troubled him. He was England's top spy-master, after all, and if there was a mystery to be solved, then who better to solve it? On that reassuring thought, he rolled over and settled into a deep, untroubled sleep.

Maggie's night was far less restful. After a perfunctory examination, Dr. Burke had returned to his rooms, leaving behind a sleeping draft, which she firmly refused to take. She didn't really think the intruder would return, but in the event that he did, she wished to have all her senses about her. She also refused Constance's offer to stay with her, or more lowering still, to sleep in her companion's room, insisting that she wasn't a child who needed coddling after a bad dream.

But once she was alone, her air of bravado fled, and she spent an almost sleepless night staring wide-eyed at the flickering candle on her bedside table, and starting at every noise. Despite the lack of sleep, she rose at her usual hour, and was sitting at the breakfast table with Constance when Captain Sherrill came striding into the parlor.

"How are you feeling?" he asked, his sharp blue gaze resting on her face as he took his seat. "You look as if you didn't sleep a wink all night."

Maggie glowered at him, forgetting her earlier resolve to treat him with cool civility when next they met. The man might have saved her life, she decided indignantly, but that didn't give him the right to make impertinent remarks.

"Why, thank you, Captain," she said, her voice as falsely sweet as her smile. "But you mustn't be so free with your compliments, else you will surely turn my head. More tea, Constance?" And she turned her attention to her companion, who had witnessed the exchange with obvious interest.

A dull flush of embarrassed anger spread across Ian's cheeks. Blast the little hellcat, he might have known she would take his remark amiss. Not that he held himself entirely blameless; as a man of the world, he was well aware of a woman's vanity, and for all her waspish ways, Miss Chambers was still a woman. Of course she would bristle at the very suggestion her appearance was not up to snuff. He would have to mend his fences, and be quick about it, if he wished to learn anything useful from her.

"Pray accept my most sincere apologies, Miss

Chambers," he said, summoning up his most seductive smile. "I did not mean to imply that your appearance was anything other than charming. I was but expressing concern for your welfare. Please say you will forgive a poor soldier his awkwardness?"

"I will if you'll climb out of the butter boat," Maggie retorted bluntly, not believing his pretty apologies for a single moment. The captain was far too handsome and sure of himself for her liking, and she doubted he had ever done an awkward thing in his life. If he was doing the pretty for her, then he was doing so for his own reasons.

"What I had meant to say was that you looked rather tired." Ian made a determined attempt at polite conversation. "Were you afraid the man would return?"

"A little," Maggie admitted, surprised he understood her fears. "I was fairly certain he wouldn't, but . . ." She shrugged her shoulders.

"You needn't have worried." Ian was touched by her honesty. "The innkeeper assured me he would post a watch on your rooms should the fellow dare show his face. I only wish I had been able to provide him with a better description, but I only caught a glimpse of him as it was."

"That is more than I saw," Maggie said, repressing a shudder as memories washed over her. "He—he attacked me from behind."

Ian heard the tremor in her voice and cursed the necessity of his questions. "Was he a tall man, do you think?" he pressed, tamping down his emotions with a will born from years of experience. "When he held you against him, did you have any impression as to his height or build?"

"Captain Sherrill!" Constance gasped, her cheeks flushing with maidenly outrage. "Please! Your questions are most indelicate, to say the very least.

Can you not see that you are embarrassing poor Miss Chambers? I insist that you stop this at once!"

"I must know," Ian insisted, shooting her an icy look. He had thought her a beautiful widgeon, and her silly protestations only confirmed that opinion. Did the witless creature not see that he had no other choice? Even if the attack on Miss Chambers was mere happenstance, the authorities would have to be notified, and a good description of the robber would be necessary if they ever hoped to capture him.

"Sir, if you count yourself a gentleman, you'll—"

"No, Constance," Maggie interrupted, her voice firm as she gave her companion's hand a grateful squeeze, "Captain Sherrill is right. If the constables are to catch the man, they must know who they are looking for." She turned to him, meeting his gaze with as much equanimity as she could muster.

"I believe he was tall, almost as tall as you. When . . . when he was dragging me towards the door, the top of my head barely reached his chin. As to his build, I cannot say, although he was quite strong." Despite her resolve, her voice quavered slightly, as she remembered her frantic efforts to free herself from his crushing hold.

The sight of the blank terror darkening her gray eyes filled Ian with a murderous rage, but it was a rage he was careful to control. Emotions only dulled the mind and confused the senses, and he couldn't afford to be distracted by such foolishness. Although he wasn't officially investigating the attack on Miss Chambers, he was still determined to do his best for her. He had never allowed sentimentality to cloud his thinking while on a case, and he would not do so now.

But even as he made the silent vow, Ian wondered how successful he would be at keeping it. He might be the consummate professional when it

43

came to his country's security, but where Miss Chambers was concerned, he doubted his ability to maintain his rigid self-control. The sharp-tongued vixen possessed the unerring ability to shatter his composure quicker than any woman he had ever met, and the realization made him decidedly uneasy.

Restraining his deepest feelings was an instinct born out of the need for survival, and the thought of losing mastery of those emotions filled him with an inexplicable fear. Perhaps it was just as well his acquaintance with Miss Chambers was doomed to be such a short one, he decided, schooling his features to show no hint of the turmoil raging within him. God only knew what would become of him should he spend much more time in her dubious company.

Any hopes he might have harbored for a private coz between the ladies and himself in the mail coach were quickly dashed when the door opened and two other passengers climbed aboard. The sight of the black-clad prattlebox and her taciturn brother brought an impatient oath to Ian's lips, and his greeting to them was coolly sardonic.

"Ah, Reverend and Miss Thomas," he said, eyeing them with a mixture of contempt and resignation, "I might have known. The morning needed only your presence to be complete."

As she had last evening, Miss Thomas accepted Ian's rudeness with every indication of pleasure. "Thank you, sir," she said, her thin lips twisting in what could only be termed a smirk. "After hearing of last night's unfortunate events, Robert and I decided we would be shirking our Christian duty were we to allow these poor, defenseless lambs to continue their journey without proper escort."

"Indeed, Miss Chambers—" she turned sharp

44

black eyes in Maggie's direction "—I cannot imagine what your guardian was thinking of to allow you to go rattling off on your own without so much as a groom to give you countenance! You must give me his direction so that I might write and let him know what I think of such an infamous dereliction of duty."

"I am a woman grown, Miss Thomas," Maggie replied, thinking that there was much in the woman's imperious manner to put her uncomfortably in mind of her former employer, "and I neither possess nor have need of a guardian. I have a solicitor to advise me, and—"

"No guardian!" Miss Thomas clasped her hands to her scrawny bosom, her eyes wide with horror. "Oh, poor Miss Chambers; I had no idea your situation was so desperate! You must allow my brother, Robert, to act for you in that capacity. Who better than a man of God to guide an unmarried woman in the ways of the world?"

"And who better to help decide where her money must go," Ian shot back, his dislike of the Thomases growing with each passing second. Or at least his dislike of Miss Thomas. So far he had yet to hear the Reverend utter so much as a single word. Not that the man stood much chance of ever getting a vowel in edgewise around his sister, he thought, his glance sliding towards the older man, who was already curled up in a corner fast asleep.

"But of course Robert would have several excellent charities to suggest," Miss Thomas said, her tone sternly reproving. "The Lord's work is never done, you know."

"Captain, I had meant to ask you last evening, but did you ever see any natives while you were posted in America?" Maggie's voice was determinedly cheerful as she addressed Ian with a bright smile. "I have read many books on the subject, and I must own

45

that I find them fascinating. Do please tell us of your adventures; it will help us pass an otherwise tedious journey." And her eyes rolled in Miss Thomas's direction lest he fail to take her meaning.

She needn't have worried, for Ian was no more eager than she to spend the entire ride listening to Miss Thomas's blatant bid for a share of her inheritance. He quickly launched into a wild, and hopefully accurate, description of the various Indian tribes to be found in America. He concentrated mainly on the tribes in the Carolinas, relying heavily on information gleaned from various dispatches and other sources. Not that he thought any of the ladies would know any different, but he preferred not to take that risk.

"How long have you been back in England, Captain?" Miss Spenser asked when Ian paused to take a sip of watery brandy from his hip flask. "I believe you said you recently sold out your commission?"

"Yes, about a fortnight ago," Ian admitted, speculating whether the pretty companion's interest was mere politeness or something more. The fetching wench had been smiling at him for the past four miles, her expression worshipful as she gazed up at him with sky blue eyes. He was not a vain man, but he knew women found him attractive, and he wondered if she was setting her cap at him. If so, she was in for a sad disappointment.

"Where are you bound?" Miss Thomas asked, her manner challenging. She had been listening to Ian's monologue for the better part of an hour, and it was obvious she was champing at the bit to take control of the conversation once more. "Home to your wife, I gather?"

Ian's lips twitched at her obvious attempt to render him ineligible in Miss Chambers's eyes. "Alas, I have never married," he said with a tragic sigh. "I've been in the king's service since I was but a lad, and never had the chance to take a wife. But now that the wars are ended . . ." He allowed his voice to trail off, casting Miss Chambers a look of obvious speculation.

Maggie was hard put not to laugh at his hopeful expression. She knew he was only twigging Miss Thomas—and succeeding, if the sour look on her face was any indication—but still she couldn't help but respond to his practiced charm. He really was the oddest man, she mused, studying his handsome profile with growing confusion.

One moment he could be as haughty as a Bath bishop; the next as suave as a London courtier. And then there was the other aspect to his personality: the hard, dangerous side that made her readily accept his tales of army life. He was still very much the officer in command, and she found herself wondering what other facets of his personality were hidden beneath his glittering surface.

"Well, if you are not rushing back to home and hearth, then where are you rushing to?" she asked, fluttering her lashes at him coquettishly. "Have you friends in Mevagissey? If so, perhaps I could invite you all to tea."

"I'm visiting my younger sister, Caroline," he said, without missing a beat. "She and her husband, Neville, have a modest estate not far from St. Mawes, and I must own I am looking forward to seeing them. I've not laid eyes on Caro since her coming out."

This much, at least, was true, and the faint hint of wistfulness in his voice was no affectation. He hadn't seen his sister, nor any member of his family, since entering the Regent's service. His break with them was the hardest part of his pose, and there were times when he longed for the sight of them. He hadn't even attended his mother's funeral, and although he knew she would have understood, it was still a pain that he felt deep within his soul.

"How far is St. Mawes from Mevagissey? Much as it shames me to admit, I fear I am unacquainted with Cornish geography. But if it's not so great a distance, perhaps you might wish to call at Bride's Leap," Maggie offered, touched by his evident love for his sister. Even though she and her brother, Edmund, had fought like the proverbial cats and dogs, she had been fond of him, and she still mourned his untimely death from influenza. Although had he lived, he would have been the one to inherit Uncle Ellsworth's fortune instead of her. How very odd life could be, she mused with a philosophical shake of her head.

"I shall have to discuss it with Caroline," Ian replied mendaciously, "but I'm sure she will be delighted. She—" The rest of his reply was lost as the carriage gave a mad lurch, sending the occupants tumbling to the floor.

Ian grabbed instinctively for Miss Chambers, holding her against him as the coach began to list dangerously to one side. He had been in enough coach accidents to know what was happening, but there was nothing he could do to protect himself or the others as the brightly painted mail coach tipped completely over, tossing them all about like so much flotsam in a stormy sea. His injured shoulder struck the curved roof with enough force to make him cry out, and his last thought before darkness claimed him was that this was a ludicrous way for the top spy-master in England to die.

Chapter Four

Maggie felt the first violent movement of the coach, but before she could wonder at it, she and the others were thrown roughly to the floor. She was aware of the captain grabbing her, and knew he was attempting to shield her with his own body. Then the world turned topsy-turvy and she realized with a kind of numb horror that they were going to overturn.

Time seemed to move with amazing slowness, and she was acutely aware of everything and everyone about her. She heard Constance's scream of fear, heard Miss Thomas's plea for divine intervention, and then a harsher, deeper cry of pain. Make this a dream, she implored silently as her head collided painfully with the side of the door; please, dear God, make all of this a dream. Then abruptly it was over, and the driver was tearing open the door.

"Be you all right?" he asked, reaching inside to help Constance and then Miss Thomas out of the coach. "Blasted ham-fisted phaeton driver ran us off the road! He might have killed us all!" He lifted

Maggie out and then turned his attention to the male passengers.

"Oh, my heart, my heart," Miss Thomas gasped, her hand resting on the front of her plaid traveling cape as she staggered about the dusty road. "And Robert, where is he? Oh, I am certain he is dead!" And she set to wailing so loud that Maggie stalked over and administered a sound slap to her cheek.

"Will you be silent!" She snapped with such firm command that the startled woman stilled at once. "Things are bad enough without you shrieking like a banshee."

"B-but Robert, he—"

Maggie spared a quick glance over her shoulder, noting with relief that the reverend was standing beside the coach, straightening his clothes and glancing about him like a confused child. "Your brother is unharmed," she said curtly, placing her hands on the woman's shoulders and turning her about so that she could see him. "Tend him if you must, but for pity's sake, do so quietly!"

While Miss Thomas rushed to her brother's aid, Maggie bent over Constance, eyeing her companion's pale, tear-streaked face with mounting concern. "Are you all right, Constance?" she asked, brushing back a strand of blond hair that had fallen across her cheek. "Do you think you broke anything?"

"My . . . my wrist, I fear," Constance stammered, wincing as she cradled her left arm against her body. "It hurts quite dreadfully, and it's beginning to swell."

Maggie gently examined the affected limb, sighing with relief as she determined it to be nothing more than a severe sprain. "Although I'm sure it must be causing you a great deal of pain," she added, after assuring the younger woman she hadn't been permanently maimed. "But we shall have a doctor examine you once we are home; just to be certain. I shouldn't wish to gamble with your safety."

"Thank you, Miss Chambers, you have been very good to me," Constance sniffed, blinking back grateful tears as she smiled up at Maggie. "Was anyone else injured?"

"I'm not sure." Maggie glanced over to the side of the road, noting uneasily that there was a great deal of activity around the overturned coach. "There was no one riding up top, thank God, and Miss Thomas and her brother appear to be none the worse for wear. I don't know if—" Her voice broke off in dismay as she saw Captain Sherrill being lifted from the carriage and laid at the side of the road. "Oh, my heavens, the captain!" she cried, leaping to her feet and rushing over to where the crowd had gathered.

Without any thought for the proprieties, she shoved her way past the gawking postilions, kneeling beside Captain Sherrill as the coachman conducted a rough examination.

"He be alive," the man said in a thick Yorkshire accent, "and no bones be broken. But 'tis a bad lump he has on his head." His black eyes met Maggie's in a measuring stare. "I best be fetchin' the doctor if we means to save him."

"Yes . . . yes, of course," Maggie agreed, willing herself not to faint. In addition to the large swelling above the captain's right eye, there was also a cut on the other side of his head, and blood was flowing freely from it, staining the dirt beneath him.

"Any others be needin' a sawbones?" the coachman asked, striding over to where the horses were standing. He had already ordered the postilions to unharness them, and he grabbed one of the bridles as he prepared to mount.

51

"Just my companion; she has a badly sprained wrist," Maggie answered without taking her eyes from Captain Sherrill's face. "We will be fine, but please hurry."

"If you are going for the doctor, I must insist you take my brother with you," Miss Thomas announced, her expression determined as she dragged the reverend over to join them. "He is possessed of a most delicate constitution, and this horrible accident has overset him completely. He must have immediate medical attention!"

"We will be on bareback," the coachman warned, his tone wary as he took in Mr. Thomas's height and rather emaciated build. "And I'll not be stoppin' for any laggards."

"My brother is a gifted equestrian, and could stay in the saddle all day if he chose!" Miss Thomas was too upset to realize her proud boast had just negated her claim of the reverend's supposed fragility. "I demand that you take him with you!"

The coachman looked to Maggie for assistance, and she nodded wearily. After bowing somewhat ponderously, Reverend Thomas threw himself on the back of a large, dun-colored gelding with a surprising agility, and the two men took off at a gallop, leaving the others behind in the dust.

Maggie knelt back beside the captain, her fingers shaking as she felt for his pulse. It was strong but thready, and she closed her eyes in weary relief.

"Is he all right?" Constance asked as she squatted beside Maggie. "You don't think he's going to die, do you?"

"Of course not," Maggie said firmly, praying her voice revealed none of her inner trepidations. "He has suffered a rather severe blow to the head, but I'm certain he'll soon be awake. And blaming me for all of this," she added with a halfhearted attempt at humor.

"I'm sure the captain would never do that," Constance said gently. "He strikes me as the perfect gentleman. Do you mean to tend him?" she asked as Maggie began unknotting the lace scarf from about her throat.

"Certainly." Maggie forced herself to remain calm as she studied the stricken man. She was no young chit, she reminded herself sternly, and she could do whatever the situation required of her. Nonetheless, her hands were trembling as she gently brushed the hair back from his forehead.

"Really, Miss Chambers, what do you think you are doing?" Miss Thomas demanded, both hands planted on her hips as she stood above them. "You know nothing of this . . . this person, and it is hardly proper that you should actually nurse him! You are an unmarried female, after all, and—"

"This *person*, as you call him, has saved my life, not once, but twice in less than twenty-four hours!" Maggie retorted furiously, her expression so fierce that Miss Thomas took a judicious step back from her. "I owe him more than I can ever hope to repay, and if I choose to nurse him, then nurse him I shall! If you don't like it, then pray stay the devil out of my way!" And she turned back to the captain.

"Well!" Miss Thomas gasped, her face coloring with fury. "It is obvious that your inheritance has gone to your head! Evidently you don't know that one cannot make a silk purse out of a sow's ear!"

"And evidently you don't know when you are not wanted," Maggie muttered beneath her breath. She wasn't usually so rude, but she felt the situation warranted such desperate measures. Captain Sherrill's condition was far from good, and she simply didn't have the energy to spare pulling caps with the troublesome woman.

Miss Thomas choked with anger and then turned to stalk majestically away, her hooked nose held high in the air. Constance gave her a worried look, and after murmuring a quick apology to Maggie, she struggled to her feet and went off to smooth the other woman's ruffled feathers. Maggie sent a brief, thankful prayer winging heavenward that she had been blessed with such an exemplary companion, and then she glanced down at Captain Sherrill.

He still hadn't regained consciousness, and she was beginning to become alarmed. Head injuries were tricky things, she knew, and she was terrified of doing anything that might endanger him. But on the other hand, she argued silently, she couldn't sit idly by and watch him die. Deciding that she had nothing to lose, she ordered the postilion who remained with them to fetch her some water, and began dabbing cautiously at the wound from which blood was still flowing.

"I don't care what Constance says," she told the captain as she bathed his head, "my luck has been abominable of late! Never mind insulting a gypsy; I fear I must have offended an entire tribe!"

Outside of an occasional groan, her patient contributed little to their conversation. Maggie continued chatting as she cleaned the blood and dirt from his face, discussing anything and everything that crossed her mind. She knew the postilion thought her mad, but she didn't care. Talking kept her from panicking, and she convinced herself that it also soothed the captain.

With most of the dirt and blood washed away, his features were once again revealed to her, and she was struck anew by how very handsome he was. He looked younger than she first supposed, no more than five and thirty, and even in repose, his face held a power and a strength that amazed her. His dark gold eyebrows were gathered over his aquiline nose as if he was frowning, and his high cheekbones and strong chin gave him an aristocratic aspect that was all the more obvious in his unconscious state.

Certainly he had the look of the gentleman about him, she thought, studying his dark blue velvet jacket and fawn-colored trousers with interest. They were quite ruined, of course, and she was wondering how she should broach the matter of replacing them when she noticed the blood seeping through the white cambric of his shirt.

"What on earth," she puzzled aloud, bending closer to examine him. "What has happened here?" There seemed to be a great deal of blood, but she could see nothing that indicated the presence of another wound. She wondered if she should remove his jacket and waistcoat, but decided against it. Not because she harbored any maidenly sensibilities about stripping an unconscious man of his clothes, but because she feared causing him greater injury.

Somehow time passed as she alternated between scolding the captain and imploring him not to die. Constance managed to keep Miss Thomas away, a circumstance for which Maggie was most grateful, and she determined to increase her companion's salary at the first opportunity. Finally, after what seemed an eternity, she heard the sound of approaching carriages, and moments later, a fashionable curricle came around the corner.

A dark-haired man with a rather earnest expression was on top, and he leapt down before it had even stopped. At the sight of the black leather bag clasped in his hands, Maggie collapsed with relief. Thank heavens, she thought, summoning up a weak smile for the new arrival.

"My dear lady, are you quite all right?" he asked as he knelt beside her. "I am Dr. William Garlowe, and when word came of the accident, I came as quickly as I could. Are you all right?"

"Yes, I am fine, thank you," she said, extending

her hand to him. "I am Miss Chambers of Bride's Leap, and this is Captain Sherrill." She felt rather foolish performing social introductions under these conditions, but her mind seemed to have shut down, leaving her unable to think clearly.

Dr. Garlowe examined the captain quickly, and like Maggie, the blood on the shirt seemed to puzzle him. "This is rather strange," he said, probing cautiously. "One doesn't usually see copious bleeding like this without some kind of obvious wound."

In a matter of minutes, the gold and blue brocade waistcoat and white shirt had been cut away, baring a wide, hair-covered chest to Maggie's eyes. She had little time to register this intriguing sight when Dr. Garlowe gave a low exclamation.

"Good heavens, no wonder he is bleeding! This man has been shot!"

"Yes, he told us he was shot some months ago while in America." Maggie moved closer, concern overcoming feminine modesty. The sight of the ugly wound made her senses swim, and she glanced swiftly away.

"Are you certain?" Dr. Garlowe asked, his brows meeting in a worried frown as he began gently probing the wound. "No, no, this is a recent injury; not more than a week old," he said, pressing a clean pad over the captain's shoulder.

Maggie blinked in surprise. She didn't doubt the doctor's diagnosis for one moment, yet why would Captain Sherrill have lied to her? Unless . . . unless the wound was a result of a duel. She'd heard it whispered that bored young officers often engaged in duels, usually over a ladybird or the like, and that the high command was quite concerned over the matter.

She glanced back down at the captain as Dr. Garlowe bound his shoulder. She couldn't believe he would ever do anything half so witless. And yet if the wound was not the result of a duel, then how had he come to be shot? What the devil was going on here?

"There, that should hold him until we reach Mevagissey," Dr. Garlowe said, looking pleased as he wiped the blood from his hands. "I'll have to restitch the wound and give him something for the fever, but he should be all right." He gave her a curious look. "You said his name is Captain Sherrill; do you know the family or how we might contact them?"

"No." She shook her head regretfully. "We met quite by accident last night, but he did say he was on his way to St. Mawes to visit his sister and her husband."

"What are their names?" He asked, signaling for two men with a litter to come forward. "They shall have to be notified; I fear it will be quite impossible for him to be moved for at least a sennight."

"I . . . I don't know," Maggie gasped in surprise. "He said only that her name was Caroline and that he hadn't seen her in a number of years."

"That's not a great deal to go on, but I suppose enquiries could be made," the doctor said as they walked over towards the curricle, where another man was tending Constance. "In the meanwhile, we shall just have to put him up at the inn. It's unfortunate, but there's nothing else to be done. Perhaps we could—"

"What do you mean, put him up at an inn?" Maggie stopped abruptly, shooting the doctor an indignant look. "I thought we were taking him to your house!"

"Miss Chambers, I am but a country doctor, and I regret to say that my house is much too small to accommodate a patient; especially a patient as grievously wounded as Captain Sherrill," Dr. Garlowe said, his expression infinitely kind as he re-

57

garded her. "He will need constant care; until he regains consciousness, at least, and probably for several days thereafter. I do have a housekeeper, Mrs. Givens, but she is quite elderly, and certainly not up to caring for an injured man. I'm sorry, Miss Chambers, but as you can see, there really is no other way."

"Then he will have to be taken to my house," Maggie said decisively, praying she would find all in readiness when she arrived. "I have a large home and servants aplenty; he may remain with us until his family can be contacted."

"But if you are unmarried," Dr. Garlowe began hesitantly, "then it doesn't sound at all—"

"Proper," Maggie finished for him, an edge of impatience in her voice. "I know, and what is more, I don't care. The captain saved my life, and I'll be hanged if I'll leave him to the care of others. According to my solicitor, there is a full retinue of servants at Bride's Leap; including a butler, Mr. Hartcup, and his wife, who also acts as housekeeper. If that isn't enough to soothe local sensibilities, I also have my companion, Constance, to attend me."

"Well, if you are certain," he said reluctantly, his eyes going to the unconscious man on the pallet. "I will give the order. It might be a trifle unconventional, but I must own it would be the best for Captain Sherrill. And it needn't be for very long; only until his family is notified."

In a twinkling the captain was loaded on the back of a farm cart that had been brought along for that purpose. A small skirmish arose when Maggie announced her intention of riding to the house with the doctor and Captain Sherrill rather than traveling in the curricle with Constance, but she prevailed.

She also succeeded in discouraging Miss Thomas

from insinuating herself at Bride's Leap, ignoring the woman's heavy-handed hints of the need for clerical supervision if she meant to install a gentleman in her establishment. Finally they were on their way, and once she was certain Captain Sherrill was comfortably settled, Maggie sat back for the ride.

They had traveled but a short distance when she became aware of the surreptitious glances being cast her way by the doctor. After several minutes of the covert scrutiny, she had taken all she could and turned to face him.

"Is there something wrong, Dr. Garlowe?" she asked, her tone faintly challenging.

"Oh, no, Miss Chambers, indeed not," he said, ducking his head shyly. "It is just that I . . . well . . ."

"Well, what?" she asked when he stammered to a halt. "Come, Doctor, you mustn't be coy around me. Just ask whatever it is you wish to ask; I shan't take your head off, I promise you."

"It is just that I am curious about you," he admitted, his lips twisting in a rueful smile. "You must know that you have been the talk of the countryside since being named your uncle's heir. We have been expecting you since yesterday, and we were beginning to grow concerned. When word came of the carriage accident, we all feared the worst."

"Indeed, why should you do that?" Maggie asked with some surprise, tucking a strand of red hair back into her bedraggled chignon. The accident had brought most of it tumbling down, but until now, she had been too distracted to give her appearance much thought. Which was probably just as well, she mused, casting a rueful glance down at her soiled gown. She undoubtedly bore a closer resemblance to a beggar woman than the new mistress of Bride's Leap.

"Why, because of the curse, of course!" Dr. Garlowe said with a sardonic laugh. "And only last week Polly Hamilton claims to have seen the ghost on the west turret. Naturally we all expected disaster to follow soon afterwards."

"I see," Maggie said, wondering if she should tell him of last night's attack. The accident had managed to push the nightmarish images to the back of her head, but now that things were calm, she found herself reliving that horrifying moment when the unknown assailant had grabbed her. If it hadn't been for Captain Sherrill, she would be dead now; she was certain of it.

Her eyes strayed to the captain, noting with relief that he was beginning to stir. His breathing seemed easier, and his face wasn't quite so pale as before. Although they were virtual strangers, she felt connected to him in a way she couldn't explain.

She turned her eyes back to the road. The sooner she reached her new home, the better she would be. She could see a large house looming ahead of them, its spires and turrets visible even from this distance. Bride's Leap, she realized, her heart beginning to pound with nervous excitement.

After years of hearing her grandfather speak of it, and endless weeks of speculation, she was about to see her ancestral home. Provided (she added with a flash of her usual irreverance), that some new disaster did not befall her between here and the front door.

Chapter Five

Their arrival at Bride's Leap was greeted with cries of horror as the pallet was carried inside. Hartcup, the estate's formidable butler for the last quarter century, was the only one unaffected by the bedlam around him, snapping his fingers and issuing orders to the scurrying servants. After instructing two muscular footmen to carry the captain up to what he called the Neptune Room and sending another footman up to assist Dr. Garlowe, he turned to Maggie with a deep bow worthy of the most exacting majordomo.

"I am Hartcup, Miss Chambers; allow me to bid you welcome to Bride's Leap. I trust you were uninjured in this morning's unfortunate incident?"

Maggie supposed an unfortunate incident was as good a euphemism for almost being crushed in an overturned carriage as any, and gave him a cool nod. "I am fine, Hartcup, thank you," she said, inclining her head politely. The action proved too much for the pins attempting to hold up her hair, and it came tumbling down about her shoulders, adding to her general air of disarray.

"I have taken the liberty of assigning you and your companion rooms," Hartcup said, not so much as batting an eyelash at her appearance. "You will find an abigail waiting to assist you. My wife will escort you." He nodded at a heavyset woman with graying hair tucked in a bun, who came bustling forward to take Maggie's arm.

"Oh yes, you poor dear, what a terrible thing to have happen!" Mrs. Hartcup clucked as she guided Maggie up the stairs. "But never you mind, we shall have you feeling better in a trice."

The rooms to which she guided them were located in the west part of the house, the opened windows providing a commanding view of the sea. Maggie paused long enough to assure herself that Constance was being cared for, and then hurried into the room Mrs. Hartcup had indicated as hers. At the sight of the room, she froze in the entryway, her jaw dropping in amazement as she glanced about her.

"This is *my* room?" she gasped, stepping slowly into the room.

"It's the Bride's Room, Miss," Mrs. Hartcup said, twisting her fingers into a nervous knot as she gave Maggie an uncertain smile. "Mr. Bigley wrote as how you might like it, but if it doesn't suit, we could easily put you in one of the other suites."

"How could I not like it?" Maggie's voice was hushed as she ran a reverent hand over the curved back of a white-and-gold-striped chair that stood before the white brick fireplace. "This is the most beautiful room I have ever seen!"

The room was large, easily three times the size of the humble room she had occupied as Mrs. Graft's underpaid companion, and it was decorated with delicately carved pieces of furniture that had been painted white with gilded trim. The Aubusson carpets were patterned with golden roses, and they stretched from one end of the spacious room to the other. But it was the bed that caught and held Maggie's interest.

Carved out of oak, the wood had been painted a soft white, and then rubbed to a satiny patina. Cupids and roses were intertwined on the tall posts, giving the bed a whimsical and yet romantic aspect. The bedcover and airy curtains were made of silk, fashioned in the deep, opulent color of newly minted coins. The thought of sleeping amid such splendor was almost overwhelming, and Maggie wondered if she would ever become accustomed to her new life.

"Is there something wrong, miss?" Mrs. Hartcup was eyeing her anxiously. "As I said, 'twould be nothing at all to move you and the other lady to another wing. The Rose Suites were remodeled shortly before the old gentleman's death, and I'm sure you'd find them much more comfortable."

Maggie cast her a puzzled look. This was the second time in less than a minute that the housekeeper had suggested a change of rooms, despite her repeated assurances that she found the room more than suitable. And there was no denying that the poor woman was decidedly nervous. She kept wringing her hands, and glancing about her as if she expected a wild beast to leap at her from the shadows.

"Is there something wrong with this room?" she asked bluntly, untying her cape and handing it to the young maid who had sidled into the room.

Mrs. Hartcup gave a nervous start. "Wrong? Wrong? Oh, of course not! It is just that these rooms have been vacant, oh, forever, it seems, and I feared you might find them musty. But if you are happy, then that is all that matters. Now, with your permission, I really must be going. This is Ann, your maid; have you need of anything, you need only ask her. Good day, Miss Chambers." And she was gone, fleeing from the room with what could only be termed unseemly haste.

Maggie stared after her, her brows knitting in confusion. How very odd, she thought, and then dismissed the matter from her mind. If she hoped to catch Dr. Garlowe while he was still with the captain, she had best hurry. She turned to the young maid, who was regarding her with round brown eyes.

"A bath, I think, Ann," she said with a reassuring smile. "And then perhaps some tea? I haven't eaten since breakfast, and I am faint with hunger."

"Y-yes, m-miss," the maid stuttered, backing away from Maggie with obvious trepidation. "A-as you say." And she darted out, leaving Maggie to wonder if all the occupants of the house were as mad as they seemed.

After a luncheon of cold chicken and fruit, Maggie took a quick bath and then donned one of her new gowns. The dress was made of soft blue merino, trimmed at the cuffs and neck with ivory lace. Upon reflection, she decided to wear her hair down, weaving a ribbon in the same shade of blue through the fiery curls. Satisfied that her appearance was all that was proper for the lady of the manor, she went in search of the doctor and his patient.

She found them in the north wing of the house, in a room the footman indicated had been her uncle's until his death. After a curious glance about the gaudily decorated room, she hurried to the bed, where Dr. Garlowe was busy tending his patient.

"How is he doing, Doctor?" She asked, dismayed that the captain still hadn't regained consciousness.

"Better, I think," Dr. Garlowe replied, wiping his hands as he stepped back from the bed. "His color is much improved, and his pulse is quite steady. I daresay we'll pull him through with no trouble at all."

She waited patiently as the doctor finished ministering to his patient, and then escorted him downstairs. Aware of her new role as lady of the manor, she dutifully offered him tea, an offer he refused with a regretful shake of his head.

"I am afraid I must be going," he said, his dark brown eyes resting on her upturned face. "I am the only physician for many miles hereabouts, and I must keep myself available in the event I should be needed."

Maggie was impressed by his dedication to his profession, but when she said as much, he gave a self-deprecatory laugh. "More like a dedication to my stomach, and to seeing my bills paid," he said, settling his hat on his head. "Please don't hesitate to send for me should the captain suffer a relapse. If I am unavailable, my assistant is more than qualified to render aid."

"Thank you, Dr. Garlowe." Maggie offered him her hand, her lips parting in a smile of warm gratitude. "You have been most helpful, as I am sure Captain Sherrill will tell you once he is awake."

He accepted her hand, but instead of releasing it or giving it a perfunctory kiss, he continued holding it, his expression troubled as he gazed down at her. "Miss Chambers, might I ask you a somewhat unorthodox question? I mean no insult," he added before she could speak, "it is just that I am concerned, and I'm not at all certain what I should do."

"What is it you want to know?" she asked, intrigued by his question and his obvious agitation.

"How well do you know Captain Sherrill?"

"I beg your pardon?" She blinked at him in confusion.

"I know you said that you only met yesterday,"

he said quickly, lest she take offense, "but what precisely do you know of him?"

"Well . . ." Maggie was uncertain how to answer. "I know he was posted in the Carolinas, and that he was on his way to St. Mawes to visit his sister. He seems witty and intelligent; all that a gentleman should be." She studied him with mounting alarm. "Why are you asking these questions? Is there something amiss?"

For an answer, he released her hand and dug into his coat pocket, extracting a knife, which he then held out to her.

"I found this hidden in his sleeve when the footman was undressing him," he said quietly, his expression troubled. "He had a second one tucked in his left boot, and I also found a pistol stuck in his right boot. Rather odd things for a *gentleman* to be carrying, don't you think?"

"I . . . I don't know," Maggie stammered, staring at the knife in horror. The handle was made of bone, while the steel blade was slender and razor-sharp. It looked deadly, and not at all like the sort of thing she imagined a man like the captain would carry.

"I thought you should know," the doctor said quietly as he returned the items to his pocket. "I am sure there is a perfectly good explanation for these, but I thought it might be for the best if I took them with me . . . just to be certain."

"Yes, that might be better, I am sure," she said. "I agree that the captain must have a very good explanation for those weapons. You asked me about his character, and I have told you that he is a gentleman. I grant you that I do not know him well, but his actions mark him as a brave and honorable man. Until he has been proved otherwise, I am prepared to give him the benefit of the doubt."

"Of course, Miss Chambers," Dr. Garlowe replied quickly, "I only mentioned the matter out of concern for your and Miss Spenser's safety. I trust you aren't angry with me?"

"On the contrary, Doctor, I find your interest in our welfare most reassuring," she said, offering him a soothing smile. "I hope we shall see much of each other once I am settled here. Good day." And she held out her hand once more.

He accepted his dismissal with good grace, and as she watched him drive away, Maggie found herself comparing him to Captain Sherrill. Both men were of the same age and build, but while the doctor was as calm and soothing as a meadow stream, the captain reminded her of the sea. Restless, ever-changing, with undertows and currents lying just beneath his glittering surface. But was he as dangerous and treacherous as the sea could be? That was the question that most troubled Maggie as she slowly made her way back to the house.

He had to run, had to hide. The enemy had spotted him, and it was only a matter of time before they caught him. He ducked behind a large boulder, his breath coming in ragged gasps as he measured the distance between his hiding place and the horse tethered to a nearby tree. How far? he wondered. Ten yards? Twenty? He tried to calculate, but his heart was pounding so furiously that it drowned out all thought. There were shouts behind him, and he knew the decision had already been made for him. He could either try for the horse or surrender to his pursuers. Taking a deep breath, he broke cover and ran towards the tree.

The sand beneath his feet was wet and loosely packed, clinging to his boots as he ran. He staggered and fell, and rose to try again. He had almost reached his destination when a man appeared almost directly in front of him. He watched in impotent fury as the other man raised a pistol, aiming it

*at his unprotected chest. He saw the flash of smoke
and fire from the gun, heard the loud report of the
shot, and then felt the icy pain tearing into him. He
was falling, dying as the black mists filled his head,
chasing out all thought, all life. . . .*

Ian groaned harshly, twisting to one side as he
fought to escape the tormenting images. But there
was no eluding the nightmares that pursued him.
On one level of his mind, he was aware of the pain
throbbing in his head and shoulder, and he focused
on it. It was agony, but at least it was real, and he
used it to pull himself out of the cloying darkness.
Sweat beaded his forehead, but his concentration
never wavered. His efforts were rewarded when the
dreams faded, giving way to a hazy sense of aware-
ness.

The first thing he became cognizant of was that
he was on a bed, but he had no idea as to where he
was or how he had come to be there. The last thing
he could clearly remember was the rendezvous on
the beach that had turned into an ambush. His
brows met in a painful frown as he struggled for
memory, but his only recollection was the ambush.
The next thing he became aware of was that he was
wearing some kind of dressing gown and that his
weapons had been taken from him, which meant
one of two things, he realized grimly. Either he had
escaped and somehow managed to reach safety, or
the enemy had succeeded in capturing him.

The thought stilled his restive moments and he
lay quietly, his ears straining for any sound that
might betray his captors' whereabouts. Nothing.
After several minutes passed, he decided he was
alone and opened one eye, glancing cautiously
about him. Good God! His other eye flew open as he
gazed about his opulent surroundings in opened-
mouth astonishment. Where the hell was he?

The walls of the room were draped in blue brocade, and the drapes flanking the tall windows were of soft white velvet, richly woven with strands of gold. Everywhere he looked there were statues or paintings of frolicking sea creatures, and the statue of a large man holding a trident, whom his mind identified as Neptune, occupied the farthest corner of the room. Seashells of every color and description littered the tops of the bureaus, and he could see a tall curio cabinet with more shells inside pushed against a wall.

He lay back against the pillows, trying to absorb this confusing clutter of images, when he noticed the headboard behind him. It resembled nothing more than a giant gilded clamshell, carved to look as if it were about to snap shut on him at any moment. Ignoring the nausea that threatened him at the slightest movement, he rolled over on his side, peering over the edge of the bed with a horrified fascination.

"Captain Sherrill!" Maggie stood in the center of the room, watching in dismay as he bent over the edge of the bed. When she heard his low moan, she grabbed the slop jar that had been placed on the lowboy, and rushed to his side.

"Here, use this," she implored, sticking the basin beneath his nose. "Hartcup will have us horse-whipped if you are sick all over his lovely rug!"

At the sound of the woman's voice, Ian started violently, almost falling on his head. He batted the basin away, cursing as pain tore through his shoulder.

"Get away from me!" he roared, flinging himself on his back. The violent movement made his head swim, and for a moment he feared he would disgrace himself in the manner she had already anticipated. He closed his eyes, taking a deep breath until he had regained mastery of himself. He cautiously opened them again, blinking as Miss Chambers's features formed themselves in a recognizable shape.

"What happened?" he asked, lying back with a grimace and watching as she settled in the chair beside his bed. He tried to recall the exact details of the accident, but they were lost in a jumble of images until he couldn't tell what was real and what was imagined. One thing he could remember quite clearly was grabbing Miss Chambers and holding her against him as the carriage began to roll.

"Some dolt in a phaeton ran us off the road; a rather commonplace occurrence, or so I am told," Maggie supplied, surreptitiously studying his pallid face. She was aching to question him about the small cache of weapons Dr. Garlowe had confiscated, but common sense as well as compassion told her now was not the time.

"I am only grateful that the accident happened so close to the village so that I could have you brought here," she continued, hoping to prod him into some sort of confession. "You are at my home; Bride's Leap."

Ian had surmised as much. The opulence of his surroundings had already alerted him to that possibility, as had the fact Miss Chambers had changed her clothing. His eyes rested on the copper-colored hair falling in silken waves about her shoulders, and he decided he approved of the change. "Was anyone else injured?" he asked, forcing his thoughts back to the matter at hand.

"Constance sprained her wrist, but other than that, we were singularly fortunate," she assured him. "It was your own injuries that caused the most concern. Dr. Garlowe was quite upset when he cut open your jacket and saw your shoulder. He says you have reopened the wound, and that it will be some days before you are fit to travel."

Ian's lips thinned in angry resignation; again, this was something he had anticipated. While Miss Chambers was speaking, he had been taking mental stock of his condition, and he had already arrived at much the same conclusion. In addition to the damage done to his shoulder, there was also the blow to his head to be considered. He knew just enough of such matters to know they were not to be taken lightly, and that unless he wished to end his days an addlepated idiot, he would have no choice but to remain where he was. The admission was far from pleasing, and some of his displeasure was evident in the harsh lines of his face.

"Is there someone I can contact for you?" she offered, noting his grim expression with mounting concern. "I am sure your poor sister must be growing quite frantic about you. I could write her a note and—"

"That will be unnecessary," he interrupted, his mind working quickly. "My visit was meant to be a surprise, and so I am not expected. I see no reason to upset Caro unduly."

"But surely she will want to know what happened," Maggie protested, mystified by his objections. "I know if *my* brother was hurt, I should want to know at once!"

"Your strong sense of family does you proud, Miss Chambers," Ian returned stiffly, annoyed that she should prove to be as obstinate in this as in all else. "But as it happens, I have a very good reason for not wishing Caro apprised of the situation; in her delicate condition, it could prove most tragic."

"Oh." Maggie blushed as realization dawned. If his sister was increasing, then naturally it would not do to alarm her. But still, there had to be someone he would wish informed. "Is there no one else I can write?" she persisted. "Your brother-in-law perhaps? Or a comrade-in-arms?"

"No, there is no one." Ian's polite smile was hard won.

"Well, if you are certain," Maggie said, surrendering to his stubborn refusal with obvious reluctance. There were a great many things she wanted to discuss with the captain, but the impropriety of her presence in his bedchamber was slowly dawning on her. It was one thing to minister to a stricken man, and quite another to carry on a lively conversation with a gentleman wearing his dressing gown, she told herself, rising belatedly to her feet.

"If there is nothing else I can do for you, Captain, I believe I shall be going. Should you require anything, you have only to tell your valet . . . wherever he is," she frowned as she suddenly noted the servant's absence.

"Thank you, Miss Chambers," Ian said, his sea blue eyes beginning to dance with silent laughter. He sensed her embarrassment and was diverted that the redoubtable Miss Chambers could be so missish. He had thought her above such considerations.

Maggie gave him a sharp look, strongly suspecting he was laughing at her. It was not a sensation she cared for, but for the moment, there was little she could do about it. Until Captain Sherrill was recovered, she would simply have to bite her lip and bide her time.

Despite the events of the past twenty-four hours, Maggie passed a restful night, rising refreshed and eager to start her day. She hurried to Captain Sherrill's room, only to find her way barred by the valet Hartcup had assigned their guest.

"I am very sorry, Miss Chambers, but I cannot let you see the captain," the tiny man whose name proved to be Samuel announced with obvious displeasure. "It will not do."

"But I only wish to see that he is all right," Maggie protested, her cheerful humor vanishing at the man's obstinacy. "I owe him my life, and as his hostess, it is my duty to see that he is receiving the best of care."

Samuel drew himself up to his full height, which put him nose to nose with Maggie. "As I am his valet, you may rest assured that his care is of the highest caliber," he informed her in the starchy accents of a very superior servant. "And I should be failing in *my* duties were I to allow such a thing. When the captain is fully recovered, I am sure he will be more than happy to receive you. In his sitting room." And with that, he closed the door in Maggie's face.

Maggie stared at the thick wood, her mouth opened in outrage. She contemplated kicking at the door and demanding entry, but such actions struck her as decidedly undignified. Besides, she admitted, turning away from the door with a disgusted sigh, Samuel would probably just ignore her.

She went down to the breakfast room, where she found Constance enjoying a solitary cup of tea. "How is your wrist feeling this morning?" she asked, taking the chair across from her companion and examining her with a worried eye. "Are you certain you are recovered from the accident?"

"Quite certain, Miss Chambers," Constance answered with a dimpled smile. "How is Captain Sherrill? I believe Mrs. Hartcup was saying that he was awake and had breakfasted."

"That is more than I know," Maggie grumbled, feeling sorely used by the day's events. "I went to his rooms to check on his welfare only to find him being guarded by some wretched little martinet named Samuel." And she launched into a detailed account of her confrontation with the valet.

"But he has the right of it, you know," Constance

73

said when Maggie concluded her story. "It wouldn't be at all proper for you to be found in the captain's rooms. There would be a dreadful scandal, and you could find yourself so thoroughly compromised that you might have no other recourse open to you except marriage."

"The man was unconscious, and suffering from a gunshot wound!" Maggie protested, vexed by what she considered to be an excess of sensibility. "Even if I were a Venus incarnate, I doubt that Captain Sherrill would be so overcome with passion he would be unable to resist my wiles. And as it happens, I'm—"

"An exceedingly wealthy woman," Constance finished for her, a surprisingly serious look in her soft blue eyes. "And Captain Sherrill, for all his kindness, is still a stranger to us. A stranger who would stand to gain much if the two of you were to marry."

"Constance! What are you saying?" Maggie set her cup down with a clatter, shocked by her companion's veiled innuendos.

Constance blushed prettily, her distress clearly obvious in the way she twisted her hands and could not meet Maggie's eyes. "I am probably being foolish beyond permission," she muttered, "but as I lay awake last night, I could not help but think about the man who attacked you last night."

"What about him?" Maggie felt a sick shiver course through her at the memory of the man's brutal arms closing about her.

"Well, doesn't it strike you as rather odd that the captain was unable to catch him or even get a good look at him? The hallway was dark, I grant you, but it wasn't *that* dark. Surely a man as skilled in battle as Captain Sherrill claims to be should have been able to do *something*."

"He did! He fought the man and chased him away

74

from me," Maggie said, more than a little troubled by Constance's questions.

"But he didn't catch him," Constance repeated, her tone so anguished that Maggie had to believe that she was sincere in her apprehensions. "He said the man simply disappeared into the darkness, and no one even thought to question him further."

"But why should anyone need to question him? What could he possibly hope to achieve by such theatrics?" Much to Maggie's horror, she found she was beginning to have her own doubts as to the captain's veracity. Also, she knew something Constance did not know. Captain Sherrill had been armed to the teeth, and if that wasn't enough to alarm her, there was also the undisputable fact that he had lied about his wound. She couldn't help but wonder what else he had lied about or what other things he might be keeping secret.

"Your gratitude, perhaps, or a monetary reward," Constance replied, rolling her shoulders in an uncomfortable shrug. "Maybe he was hoping for an invitation to Bride's Leap. As you will recall, before the accident, he was hinting rather broadly that he wouldn't be averse to seeing you again."

There was a heavy silence as Maggie digested this. As she remembered the conversation, it was she who had been flirting with the captain, even going so far as to invite him and his family to Bride's Leap. Granted she had only done so to vex that dreadful Miss Thomas, but beneath her bantering, she had meant every word. Despite Captain Sherrill's arrogance, she did have a grudging admiration for him, and he seemed to like and respect her. Or at least, she mused, her brows gathering in a troubled frown, she thought he did.

"Now I have upset you," Constance cried, blushing with pretty distress. "Papa always did say my imagination was far too vivid to be pleasing. Promise me we won't ever refer to this silly conversation again." And she cast Maggie a beseeching glance.

"Very well, Constance," Maggie replied quietly, her mind alive with possibilities; none of them pleasant. "If that is what you wish." And she turned her attention to her food. But even as she ate the coddled eggs and kippers and chatted companionably with Constance, she was busy making plans. The captain's luggage had been brought to Bride's Leap from the overturned coach, and she meant to rifle through it at the earliest opportunity.

Chapter Six

𝔐uch to Maggie's annoyance, household chores and an endless stream of visitors occupied most of her time over the next two days, making it impossible for her to search the captain's luggage. When word was out that she was now in residence, half the countryside came calling, and Maggie had no choice but to act the gracious hostess, answering her guests's rude and sometimes pointed questions so many times, she thought she would surely scream.

Dr. Garlowe was among the first callers on the second day after their arrival. He dutifully examined Constance's wrist, then excused himself to go and check on his other patient. He returned some forty minutes later, joining Maggie and Constance in the drawing room just as they were sitting down for tea.

"Well, I must say the captain is doing much better than I thought he would be," he said, accepting the cup of tea Maggie offered him. "He is a little feverish, of course, but that is only to be expected.

I left a sleeping draft with the valet, and instructed him to give it to the captain at least twice a day."

"Twice?" Maggie repeated, feeling somewhat uneasy by this piece of information. She didn't approve of drugs, as a rule, having had an employer who almost died of a self-administered dose of laudanum.

"It's only a very mild potion," Dr. Garlowe assured her with a gentle smile. "In cases such as these, rest is of the essence if the patient is to recover, and from what his valet has told me, the captain is a restless sleeper. It need only be for a few days."

Maggie wondered if Captain Sherrill would find the doctor's explanation satisfactory, but decided against further protest. Besides, she admitted reluctantly, it would probably make her task a great deal easier should it become necessary to search his rooms. Something in the captain's cold, sea blue eyes made her think he would not take kindly to such an invasion of his privacy.

These thoughts were very much in Maggie's mind later the next afternoon as she crept up to the attic. Most of the bags from the mail coach had already been unpacked, their contents stored in the captain's dressing room, but she was still hopeful of discovering something useful. A cursory search turned up little of value, but it was while she was examining the bottom of a trunk that she found a small case tucked inside a hidden compartment.

From its shape, she thought it might be a jewelry case, and she pulled it out, her interest piqued. Ignoring the dust that had somehow managed to escape Mrs. Hartcup's rigorous housecleaning, she sat on the floor, prodding at the lock with her nail until it popped open, revealing a perfectly matched set of dueling pistols. At least, that is what she thought they were, and she felt a wave of disgust wash over her that men should be so foolish as to stand ten paces apart and blithely blast away at each other.

So much for the gallant captain's talk of American snipers, she thought, slamming the case shut and returning it to its hiding place. He had been shot in a duel, just as she had always suspected. Buoyed by her discovery, she began a more careful search of the various cases, this time uncovering a shocking amount of jewelry and money cunningly hidden in the linings of each case she examined. But other than these puzzling items, she could find nothing that would give her any clue as to the captain's true identity.

She was standing there, her hands on her hips, when the import of her discovery struck her. There was *nothing*. No letters, no private papers, no mementos; nothing of a personal nature such as most people carried with them as a matter of course. Nor was there a uniform or any other military artifact in evidence. If the captain ... or whoever he was ... had left the king's service, wouldn't he have kept some small trinket for remembrance?

Admittedly she knew little of the masculine mind, but she thought any man would want to keep his uniform or his sword to pass on to his son. Even her father had left Edmund the rusting sword he had carried into battle at Yorktown! So why was there nothing in Captain Sherrill's belongings to indicate that he had ever been in his country's service?

There was no hope for it, she decided glumly, she would have to risk searching his rooms. Although how she was to accomplish this when Samuel guarded the door to the captain's chambers like a sabered Turk guarding the Imperial Treasury, she knew not. She only knew she had to solve the ever-deepening mystery, or go mad. And with this thought firmly in mind, she squared her shoulders and went down to confront the vigilant little valet.

"Hartshorn, Miss Chambers?" Samuel's dark brown eyes narrowed in suspicion as he peered around the edge of the door. "Why should the captain be needing hartshorn? He is not given to fainting spells."

"I am sure I do not know," Maggie answered, her nose held high in haughty imitation of Mrs. Graft. "I only know Dr. Garlowe suggested it might be needed. I assumed that as you are the captain's valet, you would wish to personally attend to the matter, but as you do not, I will ask one of the footmen to see to it. Good day, Samuel." And she turned as if to leave.

As she expected it would, the very suggestion that even the smallest portion of his duties might be assigned to another brought the small man scurrying into the hallway. "What? Let one of those country know-nothings fetch my gentleman his medicine? Why, I should as lief send one of the horses," he cried, outrage evident in every line of his quivering form. "They would probably accept the first thing that fool of an apothecary would try to fob off on them! Naturally I shall go at once."

"Are you quite certain Captain Sherrill should be left alone?" she asked, infusing the slightest hint of disapproval in her voice. "I thought you have been in constant attendance since he was brought here."

"I have, but as the captain is doing so much better, I am sure it will do no harm to leave him alone for an hour or two," came the smug reply. "And as I have already given him his afternoon dose, and I am sure he will sleep until dinner."

"Very well, Samuel, in that case, I shall leave you to do your duty. I will inform Hartcup that you are to have use of the carriage," Maggie replied, inclining her head graciously before moving down the hall.

Less than an hour later, she stood in Captain Sherrill's sitting room, gazing about her with a keen sense of disappointment. Like the trunks, the room was devoid of any personal touches, and she was about to go into the dressing room to ferret through his pockets when something caught her eye. Moving closer, she found a miniature handsomely displayed in a gilded frame sitting on the mantle.

Her heart pounding in excitement, she picked up the portrait and turned it to the light for a closer look. Judging from the woman's coiffure and style of clothing, she estimated the miniature had been done in the first part of the century, and she was moved by the woman's sultry beauty. Her hair was the same jet black as her languid eyes, and her pouting mouth held the seductive promise of a kiss.

Staring down at the exquisitely wrought painting, Maggie wondered who the woman was, and why her picture was the only item of a personal nature the captain carried with him. He must have loved her very much, she mused, carefully setting the miniature back on the shelf and turning towards the door. She froze in midmotion, her eyes widening in shock at the sight of Captain Sherrill clad in a dressing gown of scarlet and gold brocade standing in the doorway, the pistol he held in his hand trained on her heart.

"Ah, Miss Chambers, I wondered if you would be honoring me with your presence," he said, his voice as cold and deadly as the shimmer in his blue eyes. "I have begun to feel neglected. You have a strange sense of hospitality, I must say."

Maggie's chin came up at his mocking words. "And you, sir, have a strange sense of gratitude.

Or do you greet all your hostesses this way?" She indicated the gun he held in his hand with a haughtily raised eyebrow.

"Only the ones I find snooping in my belongings," Ian replied dryly, leaning his uninjured shoulder against the door. He hadn't drank the tea his annoyingly prim valet had brought him, suspecting it was drugged, but he was still too weak to stay on his feet for any length of time.

"I wasn't snooping." Maggie felt honor-bound to deny the charge. "I merely came in to see if you required anything when I saw the—" She broke off suddenly, her gray eyes lighting with indignation. "Why am I explaining anything to you?" she cried, jabbing her fists on her hips and fixing him with a fulminating glare. "I want to know who you are and what the devil you are doing at Bride's Leap! And don't give me that moonshine about being a captain newly returned from America either, because *I* know better!"

"Do you?" Ian decided he would lose none of his advantage if he sat down . . . carefully. He eased on to one of the blue and gold side chairs, gesturing with a casual wave of his gun that she should do likewise. "May I ask how you have come to this interesting conclusion?"

"Because you're not," she replied, deciding it might be prudent to forgo any mention of her careful search. "And I also know that you didn't receive that wound of yours in battle. Dr. Garlowe said it wasn't above a week old, so unless an enemy soldier followed you back to St. James Park, you are lying through your teeth. You were shot in a duel; weren't you?" she added with an accusing frown.

"If you say so." Ian was amused by her tactic of attack rather than defense. It was one he often employed himself when interrogating prisoners, although he hoped he wasn't quite so obvious. "What else did the good doctor have to say about me?"

"Only that you were far too well armed to be a mere soldier as you claimed, and that on no account was I to trust you," Maggie returned with relish. "And it would seem he was correct. Where did you get that pistol?" she asked, curious despite herself. "I thought Dr. Garlowe confiscated the other weapons he found on you."

"I have resources that would amaze you," he drawled, deciding it was a waste of energy to keep his weapon trained on Miss Chambers. He doubted he had the strength in his arm to pull the trigger, and in any case, she seemed singularly unimpressed by the pistol.

"You still haven't answered my question," he continued, easing his finger from the trigger and placing the gun on his lap. "Why were you searching my room? What were you hoping to find?"

"Nothing!" Maggie cried, growing impatient with his game of verbal thrust and parry. "And nothing is precisely what I found. You carry no papers, no identification of any kind; only a suspicious amount of money and jewels, and a seemingly endless supply of weapons."

"And that portrait," Ian added, his eyes straying to the mantel.

"And that portrait," she echoed, wondering why he had singled it out for special mention.

"Aren't you curious about it?" he asked, idly crossing one leg over the other. "You must be, for you certainly studied it long enough. Don't you want to know why I carry it, when according to you, I carry nothing else?" When she remained obstinately silent, he gave a bitter laugh.

"So proud, Miss Chambers? Or is it you fear listening to a grieving man pour out his heart about a lost love? You needn't, I promise you. Her name was Lynette Charboneau, a Frenchwoman of dubious morals. She sold me out for approximately three hundred pounds and then left me to die."

"Then, why do you carry her picture?" The question slipped past Maggie's lips before she could stop it.

Ian's mouth twisted into a cold sneer. "So that I will remember never to trust anyone, and to remind myself that betrayal is always around the corner. Rather good reasons, don't you agree?"

Maggie didn't, but realized that now was probably not the best time to say so. Now that he had lowered his weapon, she no longer felt so wary, and she gave him a thoughtful stare, wondering about the dark shadows she saw hidden in his brilliantly colored eyes. "Who are you?" she asked quietly.

"Does it matter?"

"I think it does."

Ian considered her reply before reaching a conclusion. He couldn't give her his true identity, at least not all of it, but there was no reason why he couldn't give her his real name. Perhaps once she knew who he was, she would understand the reason for his subterfuge.

"I am Sir Ian Charles."

Maggie frowned, wondering what she should say. He said his name with a heavy inflection, as if he expected her to recognize it. "And?" she prodded.

"You don't know who I am?" Ian didn't know whether to laugh or cry. He had spent ten years establishing his reputation as a gambler and a wastrel, and it was rather disheartening to learn that a plain country miss was totally oblivious of his existence.

"No, but as I have told you, I have only recently come into my inheritance." For some obscure reason, Maggie felt compelled to apologize for her lack of recognition. "Until two months ago, I was living in the wilds of Lincolnshire with my employer, and Mrs. Graft seldom read the London gazettes."

"You needn't explain," Ian assured her with a self-deprecatory smile. "I shouldn't have expected you to know me. My reputation is such that gently bred females are usually kept carefully away from me."

Maggie digested this. "Are you a rake?"

"And a gambler, and a ne'er-do-well, and a few other things you are much too innocent to know about. Suffice to say that it would be wiser if you were to continue referring to me as Captain Sherrill. If word got out that you had even spoken to me, I fear your reputation would suffer."

"But why were you traveling under an assumed name?" Maggie demanded. "Is that legal?"

"It depends upon the purpose, I suppose." Ian's eyes danced at her outraged tones. "In my case, decidedly not. As you surmised, I was injured in a duel—some disagreement with a gentleman about a game of cards—and although I didn't kill my man, I thought it might be wiser to disappear for a month or two."

"Were you cheating?"

"Yes, but please don't tell Mr. Allingsforth. I shot him for hinting as much," Ian answered sardonically.

Much to her dismay, Maggie was unable to repress a tiny grin. "That would indeed be ill advised of me," she agreed. "But if you didn't kill him, why must you flee?"

"Duels are illegal," he reminded her. "And there were also some pressing debts that I wished to avoid. So I simply disappeared into the country . . . or at least I hoped to do so. I fear my plans have gone somewhat awry." He glanced pointedly at his shoulder.

"Constance thinks you mean to compromise me,"

Maggie confessed, aware of the need to be as honest with Sir Ian as he had been with her. She could tell his confession had pained him, and yet he had held nothing back. In the light of such candor, how could she be anything other than completely forthright?

"Good God! Whyever should she think that?" Ian was genuinely shocked. Maggie explained, and when she finished, he was shaking his head.

"I can see why she should be suspicious of my motives," he said at last, "but I can assure you I had nothing to do with that animal who attacked you at the inn. And had I caught him, he would have paid a heavy price for daring to harm you."

Maggie believed him at once; it was there in his eyes, and in the savage cast to his face. For some reason, she was absurdly relieved, and that relief was in the smile she tentatively offered him. "What do we do now?"

"I recover as quickly as I can arrange it, and you—" he jabbed his finger at her "—will keep a respectful distance. The less I am seen in your company, the better for us all. As soon as I am able, I'll leave."

"Oh." Maggie chewed thoughtfully on her lower lip. It was an excellent plan and it made a great deal of sense, so why was she so tempted to reject it out of hand? "Will I ever see you again?"

"I shouldn't think so," Ian replied cautiously, "unless you start taking up with questionable persons. But there is something I should like to discuss with you before I go."

"What is that?" Maggie was eager to prolong their talk, for reasons she thought it best not to analyze.

"How many other attempts have there been on your life?"

"*What?*" Whatever she had been expecting, it certainly wasn't this.

"How many other attempts have there been on your life?" Ian repeated with the dogmatic persistence for which he was legend. "That night at the inn wasn't the first time, was it?"

He saw the stunned look on her face and took it as confirmation of the theory he had been formulating since the carriage accident. The attack at the inn smacked of an assassination attempt, and he could think of only one reason why anyone would want to kill Miss Chambers. The inheritance.

Maggie didn't bother asking him how he had guessed, but instead gave him a careful account of the accidents that had plagued her prior to their meeting at The Royal Spaniard. "At first I thought it was just bad luck or even mere coincidence," she concluded, peering up at him through her lashes. "I even joked with Constance that either there was a conspiracy against me, or I had offended a gypsy. Naturally I didn't really believe that, but now . . ." She shrugged her shoulder, shooting him a confused look.

"Now you aren't so certain," he said, his expression thoughtful. "Simington was a bachelor . . . wasn't he? Isn't that what made the search for an heir so difficult?"

Maggie nodded. "And the fact that he and grandfather were estranged. Great-Uncle Ellsworth entered in his Bible that grandfather had died without issue, and it took some months for Mr. Bigley to learn the truth. And of course, learning that I was the only legitimate heir to be found was particularly disappointing for him. He was hoping for a more direct descendant to be master of Bride's Leap."

"What could be more direct than a grand-niece?"

"A grand-nephew." Maggie's voice held little rancor. "Mr. Bigley was politeness itself to me, but I was left with the distinct impression that a male

87

heir would have been greeted with far more enthusiasm."

Ian felt a stir of interest. "How so?"

"A codicil to the will to the effect that if no *legitimate* heir or heiress was found, a search was to be made for an illegitimate one, which makes one wonder about Great-Uncle's morals," she added with a reluctant smile.

Ian didn't return it, his mind spinning with plans. The fact that the codicil existed meant that the illegitimate heir must also exist, and if he even suspected that all that stood between him and one hundred thousand pounds was one stubborn little hoyden, then Miss Chambers's life wasn't worth a brass farthing. He bit back an impatient curse at the thought. There was no way he could leave now. Unless . . .

"There are . . . some men I know who may be of help to you," he said, choosing his words with the utmost care. "With your permission, I could write them and tell—"

"Bow Street Runners?" Maggie gasped, her gray eyes darkening in amazement. "I should think they would be the last people you would want notified! Aren't you hiding from them?"

"Not hiding, precisely. More like I am attempting to elude them." Ian was amused by her obvious concern. "But as it happens, I wasn't speaking of the Runners. I am referring to a group of men I have heard of; former agents of the Crown who aren't averse to lending their dubious skills to those in need of assistance, and you, Miss Chambers, most definitely fit that description."

"Because I am a woman?"

"Because someone means you harm," Ian retorted bluntly. "You have been lucky so far, but your luck cannot hold. Whoever is after you is in deadly earnest, and if you want to survive, you had best be just as deadly, and just as earnest. Now, do you want me to inform them or not?" The question was rhetorical as far as he was concerned. Whether Miss Chambers liked it or not, he meant to communicate with Peter Blakely as soon as it was safe to do so.

"I will consider the matter first," Maggie answered, deciding she didn't care for Sir Ian's autocratic tone.

Ian's golden eyebrows met in a warning frown. "You'd best not wait too long before deciding," he advised her coldly. "Your mysterious malefactor has already grown weary of attempting to make your death look like an accident, and God only knows what he may try next."

"Whatever he does try will be my problem," Maggie responded, annoyed that he should think her as empty-headed as some heroine out of a gothic. Let some other female simper and wait to be rescued, she decided, tossing her curls back with renewed defiance. She was made of sterner stuff, and it was time she apprised the captain . . . Sir Ian of that fact.

"I thank you for your concern, Sir Ian," she said, rising proudly to her feet, "but as I have said, it is my problem, and I shall handle it in the manner I see fit."

Ian couldn't believe his ears. The chit had almost been crushed in an overturned carriage, attacked by an unknown assassin, and nearly flattened by a bookcase, and yet she had the audacity to stand there with her nose in the air and hurtle his offer of assistance back in his face! He was by nature a coldhearted man not easily given to altruistic gestures, and that she should summarily dismiss his generous offer made him long to give her a thorough shaking.

"You may 'handle' it however you please," he in-

formed her through clenched teeth, "but you are
going to do so with some proper help! After all the
trouble I have gone to to save your stubborn little
hide, I'll be damned if I'll let you risk it needlessly.
I'm writing my friends, and that is the end of it."

"Are you by chance threatening me, *Captain*?"
She emphasized his fictitious rank with false sweet-
ness.

"I'm advising you to use the sense God gave you,"
he replied, making one last effort to get a rein on
his temper.

"And do as you order?"

"Yes!"

"In that case, Captain, then I feel it only fair to
warn you that I never give in to threats and orders.
Especially those issued by insufferably arrogant
men attired only in their dressing gowns!" And she
stalked from the room, leaving a stunned Ian to
stare down at his brightly colored dressing gown
with a confusing mixture of fury and embarrassment.

Chapter Seven

Blast! Maggie stood out in the hallway, her cheeks flaming with color as she struggled to regain control of herself.

Once she felt it safe to show her face, she returned to the drawing room, tersely ordering a pot of tea from the hovering footman who came in instant response to her summons. She had no sooner settled down with her tea when there was a knock on the door and Constance stepped in, a hesitant smile on her lips.

"Ah, Miss Chambers, here you are. I was looking for you earlier, but no one seemed to know where you were."

"I was off exploring," Maggie replied, wondering if she should mention the captain's true identity to Constance. But after a moment's consideration, she quickly discarded the notion. Her companion knew much more of the world than did she, and there was a possibility she might recognize Sir Ian by name if not by reputation. Given that she already suspected him of ulterior motives, it seemed wiser say nothing.

"Was there something you wanted?" she asked, curious when Constance didn't take a seat, but stood in the doorway shifting uncertainly from one foot to another.

"I was wondering if I might go for a walk." Constance spoke quickly, her cheeks pinking with color. "I am feeling much better now, and it is so lovely that I have been longing to get out. The house seems so stuffy and—"

"Good heavens, Constance, you needn't explain yourself to me," Maggie interrupted, feeling a decided kinship with the other woman. As Mrs. Graft's companion, there were times when she would have sold her soul to escape the oppressive little house they had shared. "Of course you may go where you please, and once your wrist is healed, I hope that you will also make use of the stables. I believe you said you ride?"

"Oh yes," Constance said, a smile softening her features. "I adore it above all things. When Papa was stationed at Brighton, we often rode out together to see the battlements. How very long ago it all seems." And she gave a heavy sigh.

Maggie remembered that Constance had once mentioned her father had also been in the army, and that he had died while posted in America. She wondered why she hadn't said something to the captain rather than asking about the other man . . . What was his name? William something or other. Ah well, she mentally shrugged her shoulders; perhaps her grief was still too fresh to speak of it.

"In that case, we must certainly make sure you have a proper mount," she said with an encouraging smile. "I'm afraid I'm an indifferent rider at best, but perhaps you would be willing to give me lessons?"

Constance assured her nothing would give her

greater pleasure and quickly withdrew, politely refusing Maggie's offer to join her. Left alone, Maggie picked up her teacup only to be interrupted again; this time by Mrs. Hartcup.

"Am I disturbing you, miss?" she asked, hovering diffidently in the doorway.

"Of course not, Mrs. Hartcup," Maggie lied, setting aside her cup with a resigned sigh. "What is it you wished?"

"Well, miss, now that you are proper settled, I thought I would take you on a tour of the house," the older woman said, her keys jangling as she bustled forward. "I know you've already had a look about, but I thought it time you saw it all."

"That is an excellent idea, Mrs. Hartcup," Maggie approved, brightening at once. "Where shall we start?"

They started in the cellars, Mrs. Hartcup insisting Maggie don an enveloping white apron in order to protect her gown of yellow muslin. The main cellar itself was dank and uninteresting to Maggie, although she was intrigued by the large wine cellar which was concealed beneath the oak staircase leading to the kitchens.

"In case the French should come, miss," Mrs. Hartcup explained when Maggie asked about it. "Leastways that's what the old gentleman always said. Personally, I think he was hiding his French brandy from the excise men, although I probably oughtn't to say as much." She shot Maggie an apologetic look.

"It sounds logical to me." Maggie accepted this slur on her late relation's character with a philosophical shrug. "Grandpapa described him as an ill-bred tyrant with the devil's own temper, but I always suspected that was because he disapproved of Grandpapa's marriage to my grandmother."

Mrs. Hartcup said nothing, although if her loud

93

sniff was any indication, she more than agreed with this estimation of the late Mr. Simington. As they moved on through the various rooms, it became apparent to Maggie that her guide was intimately acquainted with the ancient house. She seemed to have a story to tell about each room, and by the time they reached her sitting room, Maggie felt as if she knew all there was to know about Bride's Leap and its many inhabitants.

"And what of this room, Mrs. Hartcup?" she queried as they took their chairs before the gold and white fireplace in her sitting room. "Why is it called the Bride's Room? Has it anything to do with the legend?"

In answer, the housekeeper gave her a measuring stare. "You know of the legend, miss?"

"Only what my father told me," Maggie answered with a shrug. "He says the house got its name when the young bride of the original owner jumped to her death on her wedding night. I believe he said it was during the reign of Queen Anne, although it's been so long, I really can't remember."

"It was in the last year of her reign," Mrs. Hartcup clarified, settling back against the striped cushions. "The owner, an Angus Drake, was already in his fifties with two grown sons when he first clapped eyes on poor Mary St. Claire, the daughter of the innkeeper. He went mad for her, and when his wife died, he married her and brought her here."

"How old was she?" Maggie was fascinated by the ancient tale.

"Just eighteen, miss, and pretty as a picture, with midnight black hair and eyes as green as summer's grass. She was wildly in love with a local boy and had promised herself to him. But her papa was deeply in debt to old Angus, and so there was naught else she could do."

"She was forced into marriage?" Maggie knew a

deep flash of indignation for the ill-fated girl. "That's awful!"

"Aye, miss, but more awful yet was that old Angus knew of her attachment for the lad, Thomas Trevayne, he was called, and one dark night two days before the wedding, a band of thugs set on Tom and beat him so bad, he died the morning of Mary's wedding.

"Well, naturally all knew it was Angus what had it done, but there was no way to prove it. Poor Mary went down the aisle of the village church, her face as white as her wedding dress, and her eyes as cold as death. She wed the old reprobate to free her father from his obligation, and that night before her husband could come to her, she donned her best nightrobe, walked out onto that balcony, and jumped to her death. 'Twas said she called Tom's name as she fell, to let him know she was coming to him."

Despite her pragmatic nature, Maggie felt a shiver of fear creep down her spine at the tragic story. Annoyed by her momentary weakness, she rose to her feet and walked over to the door leading to the balcony. Her fingers had barely closed around the ornate gold handle when Mrs. Hartcup gave an alarmed cry.

"Don't go out there, miss, 'tis dangerous!"

Maggie turned around in surprise. "Oh, come, Mrs. Hartcup, surely you don't think the ghost is out there and means me harm!" She was appalled the competent housekeeper could harbor such silly superstitions.

"As to that, I cannot say," she answered, resuming her seat. "But I do know that Jonathan Webster, the local stonemason, did say as how that old balcony is crumbling clean away. He says it's only a matter of time before it comes tumbling down and takes half the wall with it. That's why I cannot understand why—"

"Why what?" Maggie pressed when she stopped abruptly.

"Why your solicitor wanted us to put you here," she concluded with obvious reluctance. "We wrote him it was dangerous, even told him that Jonathan said we wasn't to go out there, but he insisted. Mayhap he thought you would like sleeping in a room what was haunted." She cast Maggie a curious look.

"It would be different, certainly," Maggie admitted, tilting her head to one side as she considered the notion. "But is it haunted? I've been here almost a week, and I haven't seen so much as a single ghost."

"Some say as it is, and I must admit that for myself, I cannot like it," Mrs. Hartcup said with her customary bluntness. "There's something about it, something in the very air, and many's the time I got the queerest feeling I was being watched." She shuddered and rubbed her plump arms vigorously. "Well, all I can tell you is that you'd not find me spending a single night in here, and that's the Lord's own truth."

"Have you ever seen the ghost?" Maggie asked curiously.

"No, Miss Chambers, but there's many that has. Why, only last week one of the chambermaids ran screaming downstairs that she'd caught a glimpse of the ghost. Scared witless, she was, and shaking so bad, I had to give her a sip of brandy to calm her nerves."

"There's those that claim she's a harbinger of doom," the housekeeper continued, lowering her voice in a confiding manner. "She left a note cursing this house and all in it, and whenever she appears, 'tis said a death will follow. It's almost as if she comes for them."

"The chambermaid?" Maggie lost the thread of the story.

"The ghost, miss," the older woman explained with a patient smile. "You see, she was a suicide and so is denied heavenly rest, and must spend eternity tied to this place. But she's lonely in death and wants company. That's why she appears from time to time, luring God-fearing folk out on that balcony and to their death . . ."

This was too much for Maggie. Even though she didn't believe such gothic nonsense for a single minute, that didn't mean she relished hearing the hair-curling tale. She had to sleep in the room, after all, and she knew it wasn't always easy to dismiss such stories when lying in bed at night.

"How very interesting," she said, her tone determinedly cheerful. "Now, I wanted to ask you about the gardens. I know it's still rather early, but what do you think about planting some roses?" And she adroitly turned the conversation from the metaphysical to the mundane.

Three days later, Maggie stood before the glass in her bedroom, studying her reflection with a thoughtful frown. She was dressed in a new riding habit of black velvet trimmed with gold braid, and although the dressmaker had assured her it was in the first stare of fashion, Maggie had her doubts. Setting the tiny hat that matched the habit on her head, she picked up her tan gloves and whip and went down to the library, where Constance was waiting.

To her surprise, Dr. Garlowe was also there, and when she entered, he moved forward to take her hand. "Ah, Miss Chambers, how charming you look," he said, carrying her hand to his lips for a brief kiss. "I rode over today in the hopes of luring you out to enjoy some of our famous scenery; how fortuitous that you have already anticipated my request!"

"You are too kind, sir," she murmured, thinking the man rather full of himself. It had been Constance's suggestion that they ride out this morning, and for a moment she was strongly tempted to tell him so. Only good breeding kept her from doing so, and there was no faulting her manners as she turned to Constance, who was watching them with a pleased expression.

"I am glad to see you are also wearing your new habit," she said, nodding in approval of the other woman's habit of shimmering turquoise velvet. "Yours is quite lovely."

Twin dimples appeared in Constance's cheeks. "Thank you, Miss Chambers," she murmured, lowering her eyes shyly. "And thank you also for purchasing it for me. It was most kind of you."

"You're welcome," Maggie answered somewhat awkwardly. She wished Constance hadn't mentioned the habit was her purchase, for it made it appear that she was fishing for compliments. Shaking off the uncomfortable sensation, she turned back to Dr. Garlowe.

"You are very generous to lend us your expertise as a guide," she said in what she hoped was a flirtatious manner. "I note you speak of 'our' scenery; are you a native of the area or a newcomer like myself?"

"I was born in Surrey, although my mother's family once lived in the area," he replied easily. "I remember hearing her speak of Mevagissey, and Bride's Leap, of course. When word came that there was a practice open here, I jumped at the chance. I have been here less than a year."

"Where were you before that?" Maggie asked,

more out of a sense of politeness than any real interest. They had left the house and were walking towards the stables. It was a soft April morning, and she paused to enjoy the damp caress of the breeze blowing from the sea.

"Oh, here and there." Dr. Garlowe gave a casual reply. "I was in Devonshire for a while, and London. A doctor must serve a long apprenticeship, before he is free to establish his own practice."

Maggie did not know that, but now that she thought about it, it made perfect sense to her. They soon reached the stables, and their mounts were waiting for them. Dr. Garlowe had ridden over on his own horse, a large gray gelding, while Constance had already claimed a dainty black mare as her own. That left the last horse, a dark bay stallion, for Maggie, and she eyed it with trepidation. She was considering asking for another mount when Dr. Garlowe said, "Good Lord, is that Tartar?"

"Aye, Doctor, so 'tis," the groom who had brought the horses out replied diffidently. "He be the best bit of blood we have in the stables, and—"

"Unsaddle him at once," Dr. Garlowe interrupted, his expression disapproving. "That ill-tempered brute is no fit mount for a lady! Bring out one of the other mares."

Maggie's jaw hardened at the casual way the doctor took to ordering her servants about. Nor did she care for his unspoken implication that her equestrian skills were not all that they should be. That this was the case didn't matter to her; what did matter was letting the doctor know that she would not be ordered about like a witless child.

"No, wait ... Clarence, is it not?" she asked, searching her memory for the groom's name.

"Yes, miss?" He cast her an enquiring look over a stooped shoulder.

"Tartar will do fine," she instructed, ignoring the trembling of her knees. "I shall ride him."

"Do you know what you are doing?" Dr. Garlowe asked, giving her a worried look. "I don't mean to contradict you in front of your servants, but I am only thinking of your safety. Less than two months ago I had to set the arm of the last stable hand to ride that devil, and I'd hate for you to risk a broken bone merely because of your pride. Are you certain you won't change your mind?"

"Quite certain," she answered, her voice much firmer than her convictions. She was already regretting her impulsive behavior, but there was no way she could back out now. For some reason, she thought of Sir Ian, and she wondered how he would react to her defiance. Doubtlessly he would pull her off Tartar's back and stick her atop some plodding, docile nag with stern orders to stay there, she mused, a reluctant smile touching her mouth.

Tartar was indeed an ill-tempered brute, and the first few minutes on his back were decidedly dicey. But when it became apparent that her will was every bit as strong as his own, the big bay turned surprisingly docile, indulging in only the occasional trick as the trio galloped across the countryside towards the cliffs. Constance had ridden a little way ahead of them, and after they had traveled a short distance, Dr. Garlowe gave Maggie a rueful look.

"My apologies, Miss Chambers, for doubting your skills. You are indeed a gifted equestrienne. Do you forgive me for implying otherwise?"

"But of course, Dr. Garlowe," she answered with a polite smile. "As you say, you were only thinking of my safety; something you appear to do with amazing frequency."

He took her meaning at once. "You are referring to Captain Sherrill," he said with a serious nod. "Has he caused you any trouble?"

"None at all." His question surprised Maggie. She had only been twigging him when she alluded to his earlier warnings, and she certainly hadn't meant to draw his attention to Sir Ian. From what he had told her, nothing could be more disastrous, and she hastened to set the doctor's mind at ease.

"He is still recovering from his wounds, you know, and keeps mostly to his rooms," she told him smoothly. "In fact, I've scarce passed more than a moment's conversation with him since the accident."

"Mmm."

"What does that mean?" Maggie knew enough of men to know that that guttural utterance often held a world of meaning.

"Well, his wounds, while serious, aren't so grievous as to require a week's convalescence in bed," he said in the careful manner she was beginning to associate with him. "He is in no condition to travel, of course, but I would think him more than up to taking dinner with you and Miss Constance."

"Perhaps he fears compromising us," she invented, recalling Constance's most recent fears on the subject. "After all, he is a stranger to us, and it is probably better that he chooses to keep his distance."

"Yes, he *is* a stranger." He shot her a meaningful look. "Did you ask him about the weapons we found on him?"

"Yes. He explained that as a soldier, he is used to going about armed," she answered, although Sir Ian had said nothing of the kind. "He apologized for any worry he might have caused us, and assures me he means us no harm."

"Naturally he would admit it if his intentions

101

were less than honorable." Dr. Garlowe's tone implied he thought her hopelessly naive. "Has he made any attempt to contact his sister? I believe you said she lives in St. Mawes?"

"Yes, but it seems she is in a delicate condition and he doesn't wish to alarm her," Maggie explained, wishing he would drop the subject. "He has spoken of contacting a friend, however, and I assume he will do so once he is feeling more the thing."

"I was thinking that perhaps it might be advisable if I were to make some enquiries . . . discreet ones, of course," he added, giving her an anxious smile. "I must admit there is something about this captain that I do not trust. He is far too evasive, for one thing, and he has told you one lie already. How many more has he told, I wonder?"

Maggie could have reassured him on this point, at least, but to do so would force her to admit to a deeper knowledge of the captain than she had already claimed. Wishing she were better versed in intrigue, she was searching her mind for some way of distracting the doctor when Constance rode back to join them.

"Isn't this a glorious day?" she called, her eyes sparkling with laughter. "It makes one want to run and run! Come, Miss Chambers, are you up to a race?"

"Perhaps some other day, Constance." Maggie felt she had tempted the fates enough for one day and wasn't about to take any more risks. "Why don't we ride over there?" She indicated a distant pile of ruins with a wave of her whip.

"The old Roman wall?" Constance said with a pout. "The ground is far too muddy. Oh, come, Miss Chambers, don't be so stodgy! First one back to the stables shall win!" And she brought her own quirt sharply down on Tartar's flanks.

The stallion, who up until now had been a pattern card of equine propriety, gave a snort of indignation and was off in a flash, racing at full speed across the rock-strewn ground. Maggie clung to his back, pulling back on the reins with gentle but commanding strength. The action did little to check the horse's headlong flight. He continued racing towards the stables, his huge body tensing in readiness as he rushed towards a low stone wall.

Maggie saw the approaching wall and closed her eyes, steeling herself for the fall she knew was inevitable. She felt Tartar's front haunches leave the ground, then there was a brief sensation of flight as she left the saddle, coming to a painful and abrupt halt in a patch of damp moss. The fall knocked the wind from her chest, and she lay there gasping silently as she tried to draw air into her lungs.

She heard the clatter of approaching hooves and then Dr. Garlowe was bending over her, his face drawn with worry. "No, don't try to move," he cautioned when she attempted to draw herself upright. "You may have broken something."

Maggie waved her whip feebly. Although every bone in her body was throbbing with pain, some inner voice told her she wasn't seriously injured, and her main concern at this point was drawing a deep enough breath to ease the constriction in her chest. Constance arrived, tears steaming from her blue eyes as she leapt from her horse and rushed over to where Maggie lay.

"Are you all right?" she cried, grabbing Maggie's free hand in a bruising grip. "Oh heavens, if I have killed you, I shall never forgive myself!"

"I . . . am . . . fine . . . ," Maggie enunciated painfully, dragging in blessed air between each word. "I . . . was . . . just . . . winded."

Dr. Garlowe took leave to doubt her diagnosis and

performed a thorough examination. When he was convinced she was relatively unharmed, he helped her to her feet. "Are you up to riding?" he asked, solicitously brushing the dirt and leaves clinging to her torn and muddied skirts. "You may take my horse, if you like. I'll understand if you don't wish to ride Tartar."

Maggie's eyes strayed to the trembling bay who was standing nearby, his head held low as if in shame. When he noticed they were watching him, he trotted over, nuzzling her face in silent apology. "No, I'll take Tartar," she said, reaching up to stroke the horse's soft nose. "It wasn't his fault I came up a cropper."

"No." Constance's bottom lip quivered dangerously. "It was mine. Dear Miss Chambers, how can I ever apologize for my carelessness? I know better than to strike a horse like that; especially a stallion. Can you ever forgive me?" Twin tears wended their way down her pale cheeks, making her look like a tragic doll.

"I know you meant no harm, Constance," Maggie replied, unable to keep a small edge of annoyance out of her voice. She ached in every joint, and although she knew it was nothing more than a foolish accident, she found it impossible to be charitable just then.

Constance gave a watery sniff, and no further words were spoken as they slowly made their way home. Maggie accepted Constance's assistance to her room, and once she was gone, she undressed and eased herself into the steaming bath Mrs. Hartcup had brought up for her. The warm water, scented with jasmine, did wonders for her bruised body, and by the time she changed into a tea gown of bronze and sea green voile, she was beginning to feel almost human.

She was sitting before her mirror adding the finishing touches to her coiffure when she heard the door to her room opening. Expecting the maid or Constance, she was shocked to see Sir Ian standing there, his face set in foreboding lines.

"What the devil happened?" he asked, coming forward to tower over her. "My valet tells me you had an accident."

"My horse ran away with me," Maggie replied, grateful he had changed out of his gaudy robe and was dressed in a simple country suit of blue serge. "I fell off when he tried taking a fence."

"Were you hurt?" Ian's eyes moved over her worriedly. When Samuel had informed him of Miss Chambers's accident, he had been beside himself with fear, an emotional reaction he put down to his injuries. Ignoring his sickening headache, he had struggled out of bed, shaving and donning a change of fresh clothing despite his valet's vociferous objections.

"I had the wind knocked out of me," Maggie admitted, her eyes flicking away from him. She had forgotten how tall he was and how handsome, and she was uncomfortably aware that his presence in her dressing room wasn't at all proper.

"How did your horse come to run away with you? Was he frightened?" he asked, sensitive to her embarrassment. He knew he should leave, but he wasn't about to move an inch until he assured himself that she was all right and that her accident had nothing to do with the other incidents.

"In a way. Constance struck him with her whip and he bolted."

"What?" His mouth tightened in annoyance. "That was a damned stupid thing to do!"

Maggie gave him a cool look. "It was an accident, and one for which she has already apologized. As I wasn't seriously injured, there was no harm done."

"No harm?" Ian stepped closer, reaching out a

tanned finger to touch the long bruise that was blooming on her upper arm. "You're probably lucky you weren't killed!"

"That is what Dr. Garlowe said," she answered, feeling disconcerted by his unexpected touch. "He didn't want me to take Tartar out in the first place, saying an ill-tempered stallion was no fit mount for a lady, but I—"

"You were riding a stallion, and a badly behaved one at that?" Ian was incredulous. "My God, haven't you enough to worry about without risking your foolish neck on a half-wild animal?"

"Tartar was a perfect gentleman." She defended her mount with growing indignation. "It wasn't his fault Constance hit him! Up until then, we were getting along quite well."

"Dr. Garlowe had no business putting you on that beast," Ian growled, realizing his reaction was excessive but unable to stop himself. "The man is an even bigger dolt than I thought him for allowing such a thing."

"He didn't 'allow' me to do anything," Maggie snapped, rising from her bench to face him. "In fact, he did his best to stop me. And I wouldn't be so smug if I were you; that *dolt* is starting to ask questions about you!"

"What are you talking about?" Ian's demeanor underwent a rapid change as his well-honed senses came to the fore.

Maggie was aware of the subtle changes both in his stance and his dark blue eyes. He was still angry, but it was a different, less personal kind of anger. How she knew this, she did not know; she only knew that the man before her was dangerous in a way she could not explain, and her tone when she answered him was decidedly cautious.

"He spoke of making a few discreet enquries

about you," she said slowly. "But he didn't say who he would contact or what he would ask."

Ian bit back an impatient curse. He wasn't worried that Garlowe's investigation would uncover anything harmful, but it was a complication he could have done without. He ran a hand through his hair and shot Maggie a disgruntled look.

"Did he say anything else?"

"He thinks it strange you haven't left your room, but I told him it was because you're probably trying to avoid anything that smacks of a compromising situation. You know how it is with you crusty old bachelors." She ventured a tiny smile. "Forever vigilant against the parson's mousetrap."

Ian's eyes flashed with reluctant laughter. "Do you think he believed you?"

"I think so," she answered honestly, her earlier anger forgotten. "But in any case, I think he may have a point; perhaps it would be best if you started taking your meals with us. Provided you're feeling up to it, of course."

"I'm fine." He dismissed his pain with a casualness born of practice. "What time shall I be downstairs?"

"We dine at seven," Maggie answered, telling herself that the happiness she was feeling was merely relief that her guest was recovering. "Constance and I usually meet in the library for a sip of sherry beforehand, and you are more than welcome to join us."

He nodded distractedly, planning his next course of action. Once he began joining the ladies downstairs, his time at Bride's Leap would be severely limited, for he couldn't linger in the house with two unmarried females without attracting unfavorable notice. He had already composed a letter to Peter requesting his assistance; now all that remained was sending it.

Maggie watched his expression grow shuttered, and wondered what he was thinking. She knew so little of him, and yet for some inexplicable reason, she trusted him completely. He might be a stranger, but she knew she could trust him with her life. Hadn't he already proven as much?

"I shouldn't have ridden the stallion." She shocked them both with her confession. "It was wrong of me."

Ian remained silent for a moment, then his harsh features softened in a smile that made Maggie's heart race. "What? You obey a direct command? Never, Miss Chambers. I hadn't known you above an hour before I knew that forbidding you to do something would be the one sure way to get you to do it."

Maggie rallied at his bantering tone. "Come, sir, I am not so complete a hoyden as you would paint me. I have been known to obey the occasional order, you know."

"Have you?" Ian's eyes rested on the bright red hair that flowed about her shoulders, and as if they possessed a will of their own, his fingers reached up to wind a soft curl about them. "There is such life in you, such fire. I do not think I could bear it if that flame were to be extinguished." And then he was gone, leaving Maggie staring after him in openmouthed astonishment.

Chapter Eight

"Are you certain there is nothing I can do for you, Captain?" Samuel asked, his voice plaintive as he watched Ian add the finishing touches to his cravat.

"No, thank you, Samuel," Ian replied, wishing the man would take the hint and leave. "I appreciate the offer, but you must remember that I am a soldier and used to doing for myself," he said, shrugging into his tight-fitting jacket of plum satin.

"Perhaps, but as a guest in our house, it is hardly proper that you should continue doing so," the smaller man responded, standing on tiptoe to smooth the jacket over Ian's broad shoulders. "I am a gentleman's gentleman, and it is my duty to assist you in whatever way you require."

Duty. The word stayed Ian's hand as he was brushing back a lock of hair that had fallen across his forehead. Duty was a concept he understood too well, according to some people, and he found himself giving the valet a speculative look.

"And were you doing your 'duty' when you gave me that drugged tea?" he asked, his tone deceptively light.

Samuel blushed. "Dr. Garlowe said it was important that you got your rest," he muttered, shuffling his feet nervously. "But I didn't give you near as much as he said I should."

"I see," Ian said, reaching a sudden decision. "Do you really want to help me, Samuel?"

"Oh yes, Captain, I should consider it an honor!"

Ian reached into the pocket of his jacket and extracted a letter, which he handed to the other man. "I need this delivered," he instructed, his blue eyes meeting the valet's. "And it is vital that no one learn of it. Can you do that?"

The letter disappeared into Samuel's pocket. "You may count upon me, sir!" he said, straightening his thin shoulders with obvious pride. "I shall see to it at once!"

Ian smiled at hearing his old nom de guerre. "Thank you, Samuel. I am most grateful to you."

"Will there be a reply?"

Ian hesitated. He had only worked with Blakely once, and that was only in the most informal manner. He had no way of knowing whether he could rely on him to come in response to his mysterious summons. Then he remembered the promise Blakely had made to repay him for helping capture the traitorous marquess Blakely had been stalking.

Although the promise had been made in Peter's languid and sardonic fashion, Ian didn't doubt his sincerity for a single moment. Beneath his urbane and mocking manner, the man was a true warrior, and Ian respected him as such.

"No, Samuel, there won't be a reply, although we should be expecting a houseguest within the next week or so."

"Miss Chambers, how lovely you look! Is that a new gown?" Constance's praise was effusive as

Maggie stepped into the library. "I adore that color on you."

"Thank you, Constance," Maggie answered, feeling as foolish as a young girl before her coming-out ball. She had spent the last three hours trying on every gown in her wardrobe before deciding on an evening dress of cream and gold satin with an overskirt of gold net. She let the maid arrange her bright red hair in its customary chignon, with a few curls escaping about her ears and forehead to soften the effect. "I see you received my message that the captain is to join us," she said, indicating Constance's gown of pearl and rose silk as she took her chair before the fire.

"Yes, and I must say I am quite looking forward to seeing the captain again!" Constance said, her eyes sparkling with anticipation. "He is ever so handsome."

"So he is," Maggie agreed, fixing her companion with a sardonic smile. "Does this mean you no longer suspect him of having designs on my virtue?"

Constance had the good grace to blush. "I hope you didn't mind my being so forward," she said, her dark lashes sweeping over her cheeks. "But truly, I was only thinking of you. Ladies in our position must take every care to safeguard our reputations."

"So we must," Maggie replied, tongue-in-cheek. "And I do thank you for your care. It seems you and Dr. Garlowe have that in common as well."

Constance gave a nervous start. "Why, Miss Chambers, whatever can you mean by that remark?" she asked, a betraying flush staining her already rose complexion.

"Merely that he is also preoccupied with my welfare," Maggie said, amused by her companion's reaction. Was Constance sweet on the young doctor? It was an intriguing thought.

"Yes, but why do you hint that we might have other things in common? I scarce know the man!"

At first, Constance's vehemence confused Maggie, until she remembered how reserved the other girl was. She had always shown a marked reluctance to speak of herself, and Maggie respected her too much to press her. Not that she intended to let the matter drop, of course. If her companion was harboring a secret tender for the doctor, then she was eager to do all that she could to foster the romance.

"Oh, only that he also rides, and that he, too, is from Devonshire," she answered, casting Constance a secretive smile. "Didn't you say you were once there with your papa?"

"Yes, but I never met Dr. Garlowe!" Constance replied, partaking of a rather generous sip of sherry. "My father was terribly strict, you know, and he certainly would not have allowed me to go about arranging assignations with strangers!"

Maggie opened her lips to issue a teasing rejoinder when the door to the library opened and Captain Sherrill walked in, resplendent in a plum satin jacket and cream-colored pantaloons. He looked every inch the proper English gentleman, and for a moment it was all Maggie could do not to gape at him like a schoolgirl with her first crush.

"Captain Sherrill, so happy you could join us," she said, rising to her feet with a cool smile that revealed none of her secret thoughts. "I trust you are feeling better?"

"Much better, Miss Chambers." Ian accepted the hand she offered him, his dark blue eyes approving of her elegant toilet as he gave a low bow. "May I say how lovely both you and Miss Spencer look? Had I known what beauty awaited me, I would have recovered long before now."

"You are too kind, sir," she replied, removing her

hand from his and moving to the crystal decanter that stood on an intricately carved sideboard. "Would you care for some sherry?"

"That would be fine, Miss Chambers, thank you," Ian answered, ever the dutiful guest. His eyes flicked towards Miss Spenser, who was sitting demurely on the striped settee, and he strolled over to join her.

"And how is our other invalid?" he asked, taking her hand in his as he settled on the cushion beside her. "I heard you had sprained your poor wrist; I trust it is better?"

"Oh yes, Captain." Constance's lashes fluttered shyly. "I hardly feel it at all anymore."

"Ah, that relieves me—" the smile he gave her was one of warm intimacy "—for I could not bear to think of such a lovely hand swollen in pain." And he carried the affected limb to his lips for a tender kiss.

"Your sherry, sir." Maggie thrust the glass into his hand, almost spilling its contents. She had witnessed the disgusting exchange from across the room, and it was all she could do not to stamp her foot in fury. She thought Sir Ian was anxious to alleviate Constance's suspicions, not add to them!

Ian thanked her for the wine and glanced around the room, pretending to notice it for the first time when in fact he had already reconnoitered it earlier that afternoon. As a well-trained spy, he made it a habit to meet only in locations he considered secure, and he was fairly certain the library held no possibility of a trap.

"What an extraordinary amount of books your uncle had," he commented, flashing Maggie another of his intimate smiles. "Do you share his tastes in literature, Miss Chambers?"

"Not really," Maggie admitted, glancing at the shelves of expensively bound tomes. "From what I could gather, my uncle and his predecessors leaned rather heavily towards Greek and Latin, while I favor far lighter fare."

"Why, Miss Chambers, never say you are addicted to Minervian novels!" he teased.

Maggie bristled at what she took for his condescending tone. "And if I am?" she asked belligerently.

"Why, then, Miss Chambers, I should tell you that even I have read the occasional gothic," Ian replied with a mild smile. "Although not, I will admit, in such eminently suitable surroundings." And he cast a mocking glance about him. "As I recall, you did say the house was haunted, didn't you?"

"Oh, please, let us not discuss such things!" Constance cried, rubbing her arms with her hands. "I could not bear to think of what I should do if I were ever to encounter such a dreadful apparition! I should die of fright on the spot, I know it."

"In which case the house should then have two ghosts wandering its halls," Ian answered with a smile before turning to Maggie. "And what of you, Miss Chambers? Do you believe in spectral visitations?"

"I believe, Captain Sherrill, as did Shakespeare, that there are many more things between heaven and hell than are dreamed of in philosophy," Maggie replied, meeting Ian's teasing look with cool regard. "But as I have never seen a ghost firsthand, I really cannot say. Have you ever seen a ghost?"

"No." He gave her another smile. "And if I am lucky, I never will. I cherish my beliefs, Miss Chambers, and I wouldn't care to have them shattered."

After dinner, they adjourned to the sitting room, where Constance and their guest played a game of piquet while Maggie looked on. Sir Ian . . . Captain Sherrill was attentive and teasing to both Maggie and Constance, convincing Maggie that he was every inch the rake he was reputed to be. But the more she listened and watched his shameless flirting with her companion, the more she became aware of a certain pattern that was emerging.

First he would flatter and then he would slip in a quick question, moving on to some other topic before his subject was aware of what he was doing. Maggie listened in growing annoyance as he skillfully interrogated Constance, pulling information from her that even Maggie did not know. Finally she could take no more and rose to her feet. Constance was her friend, and she would not allow her to be treated in such a manner.

"I believe I shall retire now, I have the headache," she announced in a strong voice that gave lie to her ailment. "Constance, would you be so good as to ask Mrs. Hartcup to send a glass of warm milk to my room?"

"Of course, Miss Chambers." Constance set her cards aside at once. "But are you certain we shouldn't send for Dr. Garlowe? You took that terrible fall this afternoon and—"

"No, it has nothing to do with that," Maggie assured her. "I often get headaches after eating shellfish, and I will be better once I have rested."

"Very well," Constance replied, and then hurried from the room, leaving Maggie and Ian alone together.

"What do you think you're doing?" she demanded when the door had swung shut. "Constance is my companion *and* my friend, and I'll not have her questioned like some—some spy!"

"If Miss Spenser were a spy, then the first thing she would tell you is that betrayal can come at any time from anywhere," Ian told her curtly, annoyed by her interruption. He had almost charmed the beauteous companion into telling him of her life before entering into Miss Chambers's employ when the argumentative witch had made her announcement. Now it could be days yet before he had another chance to question her without arousing her suspicions.

"Not Constance!" Maggie was indignant that he could even suggest such a thing.

"Anyone," Ian repeated, although he didn't honestly believe Miss Spenser was part of the conspiracy against her employer. He didn't rule it out, of course, but he didn't think her capable of the heartless cunning Miss Chambers's unknown enemy had shown to date.

Maggie continued glaring at him. "Do you really believe that?"

"Yes."

She blinked at his bald statement. "Don't you trust anyone?" she asked, feeling both appalled and saddened that he should live his life with such a bitter, cynical outlook.

"One man, perhaps two," he answered, thinking of the Duke of Marchfield and Andrew Merrick. The two men were his top agents, and he trusted them with his life. And he supposed he trusted Blakely ... at least enough to rely on his assistance with Miss Chambers. But beyond that, he trusted no one, and for the first time in a long time, the realization depressed him.

Maggie could think of nothing else to say, and after murmuring a polite good night, she went up to her rooms. Her maid was waiting with the warm milk, and she wearily accepted the younger woman's assistance as she prepared for bed.

"Here's your milk, miss," Ann reminded her, pressing the cup into her hands. "Miss Constance prepared it herself, and said I was to be sure you drank it. Are you not feeling well?" she asked with a worried look.

"Just a small headache," Maggie answered, try-ing not to grimace as she drank the milk. She de-tested the stuff as a rule, and had only requested it as a means of getting Constance out of the room. Ah well, she finished the drink quickly, grateful the bite of nutmeg hid the unpleasant taste.

After the maid left, Maggie snuggled beneath her covers, her eyes growing pleasantly heavy as she recalled the day's events. Aside from her accident and the stunning revelation that her houseguest was really a notorious London rake, it had been a rather quiet day. She giggled slightly at the real-ization. Her life must be exciting if this was her definition of a placid afternoon, she mused, her eyes fluttering closed. Her last conscious thought was that if Bride's Leap was indeed haunted, then at least the ghost wasn't lacking for excitement.

It was the feeling she was no longer alone that brought her awake several hours later, her heart pounding with fear as she lay unmoving in her bed. She blinked groggily, trying to focus her eyes at the hazy darkness that surrounded her bed. She felt befuddled and had almost convinced herself she was still sleeping when a furtive movement caught her eye. She turned her head in the direction of the balcony, her eyes widening as she saw the door standing open.

What on earth? she puzzled, her mind still decid-edly fuzzy. What was the door doing open? Mrs. Hartcup had distinctly told her that the balcony was dangerous, and she was somewhat annoyed that the door had been left open so carelessly. She started to sit up, determined to shut it before some-one got hurt, when she saw the figure of a woman standing in the moonlight.

The woman was young and slightly built, her dark hair streaming down her shoulders and over a diaphanous gown of soft white. As if sensing Maggie's presence, the figure turned towards her, one pale hand held out in silent supplication as she drifted closer.

"Come with me," the woman whispered, her lips parting on a breath of sound. "Come with me." And then she disappeared, vanishing before Maggie's horrified gaze.

Over the next three days, Ian made more of an effort to be with his hostess. Still clinging to the fiction of his injuries, he kept mostly indoors, availing himself of the house's many amenities. He told Miss Chambers that he had sent for his "friend," but rather than exploding in outraged anger as he half expected her to do, she had merely given him a distracted smile, assuring him that any friend of his would be more than welcome.

He was puzzling over her odd behavior one afternoon when there was a knock on the door and Samuel stepped in, his thin face set in disapproving lines.

"Forgive me for interrupting you, Captain Sherrill," he said with a low bow. "But there are some ... persons downstairs who will not leave even though they were told Miss Chambers was out riding. Would this be the company you were expecting?"

Ian thought Blakely could be described many ways, but he doubted that "person"—especially when spoken in such disparaging accents—was one of them. Whatever airs he chose to give himself, Blakely was first and foremost a gentleman. And of course, he would have come alone.

"I'm not sure, Samuel," he replied, setting aside the book he had been studying. "Do these ... er ... persons have a name?"

"Thomas." Samuel's lips thinned with distaste. "The man claims to be a vicar, or at least his sister,

118

a most unpleasant creature if I may so, insists that he is. They have planted themselves in the drawing room and will not leave. Mr. Hartcup is of the opinion they should be removed by whatever force is necessary, but I thought perhaps I should consult you. But if they aren't your guests . . ."

"They're not," Ian replied with alacrity, repressing a shudder of acute dislike as he recalled the verbose Miss Thomas and her equally mute brother. He was about to offer Samuel his assistance in throwing the two out the door when a sudden thought struck him. Both the Thomases had been at the inn on the night of the attack, and he had never gone back to question them.

"However, it may not do to give them their congé without Miss Chambers's approval," he said, rising to his feet. "What time is she expected back?"

"Momentarily, I believe." Samuel was frowning. "She and Miss Spenser have only ridden as far as the village. But really, Captain Sherrill, are you certain you wish these people to remain? They are . . ." Words failed the poor valet and he could only gape at Ian helplessly.

"My sentiments exactly, Samuel." Ian was unable to hold back a smile. "But still, one must do one's duty. I'll go and sit with them until Miss Chambers returns. Will that soothe your sensibilities?"

"Oh, yes, sir!" Samuel said, looking almost comically relieved. "And should they prove difficult, you have only to send for me. *I* will be more than happy to render whatever aid you require."

"Thank you, Samuel." Ian's smile widened at the thought of the little valet and Miss Thomas doing battle. "I only pray such heroics will not prove necessary. In the meanwhile, lead on. The enemy awaits."

"Well, you are still here, I see." Miss Thomas

greeted Ian with a sour look as he entered the drawing room where the two Thomases had taken root. "One would think some people would have better manners than to land themselves on others without so much as a by-your-leave."

"Some would, but how interesting to see that you do not number yourself among those well-mannered few," Ian riposted, taking a chair facing the duo.

Leonora drew herself upright. Like before, she was attired all in black, her hair pulled back so tightly that Ian wondered she could blink. "We were sent here by God," she informed him in a voice that fairly dripped with self-righteous pride. "What other invitation do we need?"

"What other indeed," Ian replied, a niggling suspicion beginning to tug at his mind.

"Did the Almighty have a specific reason why you should visit Miss Chambers?" he asked, leaning back in his chair and surveying the two with cool, unwavering eyes. "Or is that a secret you wish to reveal only to her?"

"Spirits."

Ian frowned at Miss Thomas's thin-lipped response. "I beg your pardon?"

"Spirits," Miss Thomas repeated as if he were the slowest top alive. "Evil spirits, to be exact. Dearest Robert—" she cast a fond look at her brother, who was making steady inroads in the small tea the footman had grudgingly fetched "—and I were staying with a nearby vicar when word came to us that an unholy presence has been seen walking these very halls, and we are come to drive it out."

Ian's jaw clenched with the effort not to laugh aloud. "Unless you are referring to me—" he gave her a cutting smile "—then you must be speaking of the resident ghost."

"An evil Jezebel who committed the most unnatural of crimes," Leonora cried, her dark eyes ablaze with religious fervor. "Is it any wonder the wretched creature walks the night, attempting to lure the living out into the eternal darkness where she herself dwells? Well, she shall not succeed with Miss Chambers! I shall see to that, even if it means I must face the Prince of Evil himself!"

Ian disregarded most of this dramatic pronouncement, seizing on the one item of interest. "What about Miss Chambers?" he demanded, all sense of humor leaving him.

Whatever Miss Thomas might have said in response was lost as Maggie and Constance chose that moment to enter. Judging from the pained smile on her face, Ian knew she had been forewarned of the Thomases' presence, a theory that was proven correct as she said, "Miss Thomas, the butler told me you and your brother were here. What a pleasant surprise to see you again." She nodded at the reverend, who paused stuffing his face long enough to scramble to his feet for a jerky bow.

"As I was telling the captain here—" Leonora shot Ian a poisonous look "—once I heard of the danger to your immortal soul, I could not stay away! I hope I may know my duty as well as the next woman, and whatever the danger to myself, I knew I could not rest until we had saved you from the powers of darkness."

"The ghost," Ian explained at Maggie's look of confusion. "It seems God has been telling Miss Thomas all about Bride's Leap's nocturnal visitor."

Maggie paled, feeling a wave of cold horror washing over her. She had tried convincing herself that the specter she had seen that night was nothing more than a figment of her imagination; the remnant of a dream she could not remember. Her wide gray eyes went to Miss Thomas. "How did you—"

"It wasn't God." The older woman was scowling

121

at Sir Ian. "It was Becky, the Underwoods' maid. Her cousin Polly is the scullery maid here, and she says the ghost was seen quite clearly only a few days ago, and seen on your balcony, Miss Chambers, is that not so?" Black eyes regarded her with open challenge, as if daring her to refute the charges.

"Yes, but I still don't see how—" Maggie began, only to be interrupted by both Constance and Sir Ian.

"Oh, poor Miss Chambers, you must have been terrified!" her companion cried, while Sir Ian looked as if he could cheerfully break something.

"What? Why the devil didn't you tell me? How long has this nonsense been going on?"

"It's not nonsense!" Maggie snapped, her gray eyes sparkling with indignation as she glared at him. "And as for why I didn't tell you, I believe you have just answered your own question. Why should I tell you anything and open myself to your ridicule? Besides—" her lips thrust forward in an angry pout "—I only saw it the one time."

There was a great deal of talk after this, with each person demanding a description of what she had seen. Maggie complied reluctantly, casting Sir Ian occasionally defying looks as she told them of the ghostly figure she had glimpsed that night. When she was finished, Miss Thomas was fairly quivering with excitement.

"A true emissary of darkness!" she cried, clapping her hands in joy. "We have come not a moment too soon, I am sure of it! We must act quickly if we mean to thwart it before it achieves its evil intent."

"And what precisely do you mean to do?" Ian asked, his eyes resting on Miss Thomas's hair. It was an uncertain shade of brown, he noted, but in the moonlight, would it not have appeared black, especially to a mind as conditioned as Miss Chambers's had been? He thought it more than passing strange that these bizarre episodes seemed to happen whenever the Thomases were anywhere about.

"We shall perform a rite of exorcism!" Leonora announced with relish. "If those heathen papists think they can drive out evil spirits with all their mumbo jumbo, only think what we might do!"

Maggie was intrigued, despite her fear of appearing foolish in front of Sir Ian. She didn't believe for one moment that Miss Thomas and her brother possessed any heavenly powers, but on the other hand, how could it hurt? She doubted she could endure another night of starting nervously at every shadow.

"What would we have to do?" she asked, ignoring Sir Ian's snort of disgust.

"First we shall hold a séance and contact the creature's spirit," Miss Thomas explained, her plain countenance lit by an eager smile. "And then we invoke God's name and order her to depart this earthly plane."

"Is that all?" Maggie was faintly disappointed. She had been hoping for something a trifle more dramatic.

"Well, we could conduct a search, I suppose." Miss Thomas bit her lip uncertainly. "This is a large house, and if we could find the point at which the strongest emanations occur, we could bless it and thereby drive the creature out."

"But—" Maggie's protest was automatic.

"An excellent suggestion!" Ian exclaimed, surprising all in the room. He had been sitting there listening in mounting repugnance to Miss Thomas's ludicrous prattle until she mentioned a search. Ian didn't believe in such things as spirits and shades; there was a human intelligence at work here, and he knew it. He also knew the ghost's appearance was tied somehow to the threat to Miss Chambers, but the only way he could prove it would be to trap the person or persons he felt most likely responsible for the ghost's sudden appearance.

A search was a risky proposition at best, but if all went as he planned, the villains would soon be unmasked. He had played far more dangerous games in his day, he reminded himself grimly, and he had won. The Thomases might think themselves clever, but they were about to learn what it meant to cross swords with a true master of the game.

Pinning a cool smile on his face, he cast the other four people in the room a superior look.

"When do we start?"

Chapter Nine

Maggie was the first to speak in the stunned silence that followed his announcement. "We are serious about this, Captain," she warned, her expression frankly skeptical as she studied him. "If you mean to laugh up your sleeve at us . . ."

"On the contrary, Miss Chambers, I am in complete agreement with Miss Thomas," he said, his tone lofty. "A search for . . . er . . . emanations is definitely in order. I do not care for the thought of spirits, restless or otherwise, roaming the halls while I sleep."

"But the ghost appeared on the balcony," Maggie protested, not quite believing Sir Ian's sudden determination to go ghost hunting, "and we can't possibly go out there!"

"Whyever not?" Leonora wanted to know. "*I* am not afraid of the powers of darkness!"

"Perhaps not, but you might sing a different tune when you find the floor crumbling away beneath you," Maggie said, repeating all that Mrs. Hartcup had told her of the balcony's dangerous condition.

"Well, perhaps in that case, it might be better if

we remain in the bedchamber itself, rather than venturing outside," Leonora decided, looking slightly green. "Robert isn't overly fond of heights."

They spent the next half hour discussing their plans and were about to set out when Dr. Garlowe arrived. Upon hearing of the search, he pleaded to be included, a circumstance Ian was quick to turn to his own advantage.

"A physician is the very thing we need in case one of the ladies should swoon," he announced, ignoring the glares the three ladies shot him. "And another gentleman will even out the numbers. We shall split up and search the house in teams. Miss Thomas and her brother shall begin with the attic; Dr. Garlowe, you and Miss Spenser may take the inhabited part of the house, while Miss Chambers and I investigate the cellars."

"I think it better that my brother accompany Miss Chambers," Leonora countered, fixing Ian with a fishy stare. "As she is the one most threatened by these disturbances, she is the one in most need of divine protection. I shall accompany you."

Ian could have cheerfully throttled the tiny woman. Part of the reason he had agreed to this ridiculous charade in the first place was so that he could slip away at some provident moment and spy unseen on the others. That would be difficult if not impossible to accomplish with Miss Thomas clinging to his side like a limpet; nor did he relish the prospect of Miss Chambers wandering about a darkened cellar accompanied by a man he strongly suspected of meaning her harm.

"I do not think that advisable," he began, abandoning his pose as a genial guest and allowing the full weight of his personality to show. "If there is danger, I am the one most equipped to deal with it."

"Nonsense." Leonora gave a loud snort. "Of what

use would your braggadocio be against a ghost? She is safer with Robert. At least *he* is a man of God!"

"She is coming with me."

"You are too kind, Captain, but I believe I will go with Reverend Thomas," Maggie said quickly, anxious to avoid the full-scale war she sensed was brewing. Besides, she found the notion of Sir Ian being dragged about by Miss Thomas diverting, and she was unable to resist pairing them together.

Ian cast her a furious look, his jaw hardening with temper. In light of her refusal, there was little he could do without alerting the Thomases, but later, he vowed, he would have a word or two with his mischievous hostess.

"How very dusty this place is," Maggie said to Reverend Thomas some twenty minutes later as they crawled about the main cellar. "I am sure my ghost was never down here; her gown was far too white."

The reverend's noncommittal grunt brought a smile to her face, and she wondered how Sir Ian and Miss Thomas were faring. The last she saw of them, the woman was quoting Scriptures at him, imperiously prodding him along as they went up the stairs. She supposed it was wrong of her to play such a shabby trick on him, especially as he was doing his best to help her, but she had been unable to stop herself. Any man who acted like such an ice-blooded autocrat deserved to be taken down a peg or two, she decided, stepping around the corner to get a better look at the wine cellar she had only glanced at during her tour with Mrs. Hartcup.

The ancient door was unlatched and she pushed it open with the palm of her hand, hesitating when the feeble light from her candle failed to penetrate the stygian darkness. She was about to call for Brother Thomas when, for some reason, she thought

127

of Sir Ian. How he would smile to see her behaving in such a typically feminine fashion, she thought, and that was enough to send her striding boldly forward. She had barely taken three steps when the ground suddenly disappeared from beneath her feet, sending her plunging headlong into the blackness.

For several seconds she was so startled by the fall and the loss of her candle that she was unable to move, lying on the cold dirt floor with her heart pounding in her chest. Gradually her fright diminished and she sat up, wincing at the various aches and pains in her body.

Without her candle, the room was completely black, and she had to use her hands to guide her towards the door. She also discovered the reason for her fall. The floor was slanted, doubtlessly to facilitate loading and unloading casks of wine, she decided, breathing a sigh of relief as her fingers located the rough wooden planks of the door. Discovering it had somehow shut and locked behind her didn't even alarm her at first. After all, Brother Thomas had been right behind her, and she had only to pound on the door and call his name to be rescued. But when no one came in response to her cries, she began to grow uneasy.

Every one of her childhood fears, from a dread of spiders to a choking terror of the dark, came back to taunt her, and it was all she could do to keep from dissolving into hysterics. Only the thought of Sir Ian kept her from disgracing herself, and she clung to the knowledge that he would somehow find her. She didn't know why she knew this, she simply did, and she hugged that thought to her chest, using it as a talisman to keep the horror at bay.

She had no way of knowing how long she sat there, but finally there was a rap on the door and a familiar voice was calling out her name.

"Miss Chambers? Maggie? Are you in there?"

"Ian!" His true name burst unbidden from her lips as she struggled awkwardly to her feet. "I'm locked in," she shouted, blinking back tears as relief washed over her.

There was a metallic rattle and then Ian said, "The latch is rusted. Stand back, we're going to have to force it."

Maggie did as she was ordered, shaking as reaction to her harrowing experience set in. While she had thought herself in danger, she had managed to keep her emotions firmly in check, but now that rescue was close at hand, she found her control disintegrating. She could only stand there, trembling with emotion, as the door flew open.

"What the devil are you doing in here?" her rescuer demanded, his disapproving features illuminated by the torch he was holding aloft. "Are you aware we have been searching for you for the better part of an hour?"

The words of gratitude Maggie had been about to utter withered on her lips, and she glared at him instead. "I'm aware that I've been sitting in this rat-infested hole for what seems like an eternity," she snapped, noting that the others had joined Sir Ian and were regarding her with a variety of emotions evident on their faces. "What kept you so long? I might have died down here!"

Ian returned her glare full measure. When he had learned she was missing, he had been like a man possessed, taking personal charge of the search with such determination that none had dared question his authority. He had envisioned every conceivable kind of mishap that might have overtaken her, from a fall down a staircase to being carried off by some unknown agent. Finding her safe and sitting as snug as a nun at vespers turned his raw anxiety into fury, and it was all he could do to stop himself from giving her a sound shaking. He might have known the little vixen would be unable to resist causing such mayhem, he fumed, making a Herculean effort to regain control of his emotions.

"We might have found you sooner had you made us aware of your location," he said, his voice fairly dripping with icy disdain. "Did it never occur to you to cry out or pound on the door so as to guide us to you?"

"Oh, it occurred to me, all right," she replied sweetly, holding up her scraped palms for his inspection. "But when no one came, I gave up after the first thirty or so minutes."

The sight of raw flesh brought a gasp to Ian's lips, but before he could move, Dr. Garlowe was brushing him aside, his tone solicitous as he slipped an arm about Maggie's shoulders and began guiding her out into the passageway.

"Dear Miss Chambers, you must come with me while I tend your poor hands!"

Happy that someone at least seemed pleased to see her, Maggie allowed the doctor to help her up the stairs and into the parlor. The others trailed at their heels, and while he cleaned and bandaged her hands, she told them of her ordeal.

"Well," Leonora said after Maggie had finished speaking, "this confirms my worst fears. You are clearly the intended victim of this evil shade, Miss Chambers, and drastic steps must be taken if we are to save your immortal soul." She straightened her bony shoulders, her face taking on a martyr's glow. "I shall move in at once."

This was too much for Maggie. She didn't mind playing the invalid to plague Sir Ian, but there were limits to what she was willing to do for simple revenge. "I should hardly think the steps we take need to be quite that drastic," she said, ignoring her houseguest's smug grin. "I am sure my accident had nothing to do with the ghost. It was just an unfortunate mishap, that is all."

"Unfortunate mishaps seem to be a habit with you," Leonora retorted with a knowing look. "First the attack at the inn, then the carriage accident, and now this. You must own it is more than passing strange, and—"

"What attack at the inn?" Dr. Garlowe interrupted, his expression growing increasingly horrified as Leonora gave her wild and somewhat inaccurate account of the evening's events.

"So you see," she concluded with obvious relish, "a demonic influence is clearly at work here, and we must look sharp if we are to triumph in the end. It will be a hardship, but Robert and I are used to hardships, aren't we, dearest?" She glanced at her brother, who was busy fortifying himself with the contents of the brandy decanter.

There was no answer, and taking his silence as obvious confirmation, Leonora rose to her feet. "We must make arrangements with our other hostess, but we should be returning within a day or two. In the meanwhile, I urge you to sleep with the Good Book close at hand, and should this hussy dare show her face again, you might try quoting some verses at her."

"No, really, Miss Thomas, you mustn't trouble yourself," Maggie protested, realizing that she was losing the battle to keep the other woman out of her house.

"Oh, it's no trouble," she was assured. "And as I have said, it is our Christian duty to help you in this time of spiritual crisis."

"But—"

"No, no thanks are necessary," Leonora said, waving her hand magnanimously. "Come, Robert, 'tis time we were going." And with that, she was

131

gone, sweeping from the room before Maggie could think of the words to stop her.

It was late the next afternoon before Peter arrived, accompanied by a footman, a valet, and what seemed a mountain of baggage.

"What? No cook?" Ian asked sardonically as he watched the other man supervising the unloading of his wardrobe.

"Well, your note did say it was an emergency," Peter Blakely replied, indicating where he wanted a certain pile of cravats to go. "And I didn't think there was time to fetch her back from Surrey, where she has gone to visit her sister. Besides, unlike Robert and James, Mrs. Fuston is of no use whatsoever in a good fight; although there are some who claim her Yorkshire pudding constitutes a lethal weapon."

Ian's mouth lifted in a smile at Peter's drawling words. Had he not been warned by Marchfield not to be taken in by the red-haired dandy's indolent air and affected manners, he might have been concerned in his choice of confederates. Then Peter turned to face him, and in his dark blue eyes he saw a familiar hardness.

"The solicitor checks out as clean as the first snow of winter. No debts, and no unexplained sources of income. I think we can safely rule him out at this point."

Ian shifted uneasily, his eyes flicking to the two servants, who went about their business, seemingly oblivious to the unusual conversation. Peter followed the direction of Ian's gaze and smiled slightly.

"His Grace warned me of your dislike of servants, Sir, but I can assure you that you may trust either Robert or James with your life. Both have served in the army, and I will personally vouchsafe for their discretion."

"What about the innkeeper?" Ian asked, tacitly accepting the other two men. "I thought he had a sly look about him."

"He's known to be on the quick side, and more than one barrel of smuggled rum has been traced to his establishment," Peter said, ticking off the information he had uncovered. "It's well-known that he's not very particular how he makes his money, and he's wonderfully susceptible to a bribe."

"Then he was involved in the attack on Miss Chambers?"

"No, he is a blackguard, but not an out-and-out villain. Besides, he'd have to be a fool to consent to the murder of a guest in his own establishment."

Ian conceded this point. "What about the carriage? Was it ever ordered?"

Peter shook his head, his expression thoughtful. "Not as far as I was able to discern, and I inquired at every stable within a fifteen-mile radius."

"And you claim the solicitor is innocent?" Ian's brows met in an angry frown. "He allegedly ordered the damned carriage, and the fact that he did not seems to implicate him rather strongly in my books."

"I agree, but again, there is no other proof that he is involved, and his reputation is impeccable."

"We are talking of a fortune of over one hundred thousand pounds, Blakely," Ian reminded him coolly. "And that could make a better man than Mr. Bigley cast aside more than his self-respect. Even if he isn't acting purely for himself, that isn't to say he isn't acting for someone else."

"The mysterious heir." Peter nodded in agreement. "That seems the most likely scenario, I grant you. Any suspects?"

"No," Ian admitted reluctantly. "I have been too

busy trying to keep Miss Chambers in one piece; a far from easy task, I assure you."

"A hellion, is she?" Peter looked pleased. "Excellent, I cannot abide well-behaved ladies; they bore me to flinters. Which reminds me, where is my hostess? I was somewhat disappointed she wasn't here to greet me."

"Riding." Ian's clipped response brought a knowing grin to Peter's face.

"Am I to take it you disapprove?"

"The last time she tried it, she was almost killed!" Ian growled, his expression sour. "Not content with having some unknown villain stalking her, she insisted on riding the most vicious animal in the entire stable, and it ran away with her. She was thrown when the damned beast took a fence."

"And you are certain it was an accident?"

"Yes, her fool of a companion hit it with her crop."

"Mmm." Peter rubbed a finger down his nose. "Well, I can certainly see why you are upset at the thought of her venturing out again. Are there any other developments I should know about?"

Ian told him about the ghost hunt and its aftermath, and the younger man shot him an outraged look.

"And you didn't wait for me? Really, Sir, that is hardly sporting of you! You might have known I would want to be included."

"I apologize." Ian was hard put not to laugh at Blakely's petulant expression. "But the decision wasn't mine. Miss Thomas had the little drama well orchestrated, and there was naught I could do but go along." He went on to describe his suspicions regarding the Thomases, and by the time he finished, Peter was nodding in agreement.

"I agree they do bear closer scrutiny, and I promise to get right on it. Unless you have already done so?" He glanced questioningly at Ian.

"No, as I explained, I am supposed to be 'resting,' and my usual lines of communication are temporarily closed. Besides—" he shrugged his shoulders "—this is hardly the Crown's concern."

"No, it's not," Peter replied, a faintly speculative gleam entering his eyes. "Which makes one wonder why you have chosen to involve yourself in this gothic farce."

Ian had no answer to give him. It was a question he had asked himself more than once, and he was no closer to finding a solution. In the beginning he told himself it was because it was his duty, and to a certain extent, that was so. He also told himself he was involved because he was the best man for the job, and again, that was part of the truth. But only part of it. The rest of the truth did not bear thinking of.

Maggie returned from her ride some two hours later, and upon learning of her guest's arrival, she dashed up to change into a gown of emerald voile before joining them in the drawing room. "My apologies for not being present when you arrived, Mr. Blakely," she said, smiling sweetly as she offered him her hand. "What a terrible hostess you must think me."

"Not at all, Miss Chambers." Peter's blue eyes danced with laughter as he bowed over her hand. "Guests who arrive at their own leisure mustn't expect their hostess to dance attendance upon them."

"Where is Miss Spenser?" Ian asked, his eyes narrowing at the sight of the two redheads smiling at each other. They were so alike in appearance, they might have been mistaken for brother and sister, and he had to admit they made a striking couple.

"She is changing, but should be joining us shortly," Maggie replied, accepting Peter's hand as she took her chair.

"Then we had best speak fast while we have the privacy." Ian thrust his troubling emotions aside as he picked up the familiar reins of command. "I have already briefed Blakely on what has transpired, or at least as much of it as I know." Here he shot her a suspicious look. "Is there anything you would like to add?"

"Only that I can't imagine why anyone should wish me harm," she answered truthfully, ignoring the clipped command in his voice. "What could they possibly have to gain?"

"Your inheritance, of course," Peter replied, crossing one elegantly shod foot over the other. "And you needn't cast daggers at me, Sir," he added, shooting Ian a lazy smile. "It's past time the chit was told."

Maggie was about to take exception to being called a chit when the significance of Mr. Blakely's remark suddenly occurred to her. "The inheritance?" she echoed, turning confused gray eyes to Ian. "But I don't understand how that can be. I told you, I am the only heir left!"

"The only *legitimate* heir," Ian clarified through clenched teeth, furious that Blakely had been so forthcoming. He would have preferred keeping such suspicions to himself; at least until he had further proof. "The codicil to your great-uncle's will seems to indicate such a person may exist, and if he does . . ." He didn't bother completing the sentence.

Maggie sat back in her chair, a feeling of cold horror washing over her. It had been bad enough to be the target of some unknown madman, but to learn there was someone out there with a very real reason for wanting her dead shocked her to the very marrow of her bones. She lifted her eyes to Ian's harsh face. "Who is it?"

"I don't know, Maggie," he said, using her Christian name for the first time. "But I fear it may be someone close to you. And I'll find him; I swear to God, I shall find him."

"And I will help." Peter's vow was just as determined as Ian's. "But first we must need explain my presence here. What have you told the others about me?"

"Only that you are Sir Ian . . . Captain Sherrill's friend and that you have come to take him home," she said, shaking off her feelings of shock and confusion. "But how am I to introduce you? Will you be using your own name, or like the captain, are you traveling sub rosa?"

Peter gave a wicked grin. "By my own name, if you please. Unlike Sir, I have no affinity for disguises, and I am much too vain to allow another to accept credit for my heroic deeds."

Despite the seriousness of the situation, Maggie couldn't help but smile. "Have there been so many?"

"Oh, dozens," came the airy reply as Peter flicked an invisible piece of lint from the sleeve of his bottle green jacket. "Not nearly as many as Sir, but I like to think I do my humble best."

Maggie was intrigued by his answer and the fact that Mr. Blakely had referred to Sir Ian simply as "Sir." She had a feeling that the name held some special significance, but before she could comment on it, Constance came hurrying into the room, looking flushed and lovely in a ruffled tea gown of rose muslin.

"I am sorry if I kept you waiting," she said once the introductions had all been made. "I trust you had a safe journey from London, sir?" She fluttered her thick lashes at Peter.

"A journey from London is tedious by its very description, dear lady," he replied in his languid fashion, raising his teacup to his lips. "I have always found the provinces weary beyond bearing, and I wouldn't be here now if it hadn't been for the urgent missive my friend Marcus sent me. But really, old boy, I fail to see why you are in such a dashed hurry to leave. Had I landed in such a bevy of lovely ladies, I should never wish to be rescued."

"Nor would I, had I any say in the matter," Ian replied with a smile every bit as flirtatious as Peter's. "But alas, duty calls."

"Duty." Peter shuddered in distaste. "Come, lad, that is something you should have cast off along with your colors. You're not in the army now, and 'tis time you had a bit of fun. Don't you agree, Miss Spenser?" He turned to Constance for confirmation.

"I am sure a strong sense of duty is always admirable in a gentleman, Mr. Blakely," she replied, her lips pressing together in a reproving smile.

"Ah, I had forgotten you were a general's daughter," Peter said with a tragic sigh. "Now I suppose I am quite in your black books for my dilettante ways."

Not irretrievably so," Constance said with a laugh. "And my father, sir, was but a colonel."

"Colonel, general, really it is so hard to tell with all those medals and pretty decorations. I have often thought the army most dreadfully overdressed, although I daresay that isn't something I should be confessing to a true daughter of the regiment." He cast her a teasing look.

"I will try not to mention it to Papa," Constance said, turning her attention to Ian, who was watching Peter's antics with carefully disguised interest. "But when will you be leaving, Captain Sherrill? How sad to think we are to be parted so soon when we have scarce had time to get to know each other."

"With Dr. Garlowe's permission, I had hoped to leave within the week," Ian answered smoothly, shooting Maggie a warning look. "Although now I suppose we shall have to wait until after the dinner party."

"Dinner party?" Constance's brow pleated in confusion.

"The one Miss Chambers insists upon holding in my honor," he explained, not batting a lash at the lie. "I have tried talking her out of it, but to no avail. Perhaps you might have better luck convincing her, Miss Spenser."

"I fear that like Mr. Blakely, you have chosen the wrong ally, Captain." Maggie didn't betray her surprise by so much as an inch. "I am sure that Constance agrees with me that your bravery deserves recognition. Don't you, Constance?"

"But of course I do," Constance agreed swiftly. "And how very like you, dear Miss Chambers, to want to do such a generous thing. I only wish you might have said something earlier so that I might have helped you with the planning."

"As I still have invitations to write and menus to plan, you may be quite sure I shall take you up on your offer," Maggie said, wondering if she would have enough time to pull off the bogus party.

The topic of the party and who they would invite saw them through the next hour, and then Constance was rising to her feet, casting the others an apologetic smile as she took her leave. "I pray you will excuse me, but I am feeling rather weary, and believe I shall retire to my rooms. With your permission, Miss Chambers?"

"Of course, Constance," Maggie said, feeling a twinge of guilt at lying to her friend. She would have liked to confide in her about the party, but her good sense told her Sir Ian would rail at the very thought. He really was the most suspicious man, and Mr. Blakely, for all his fine airs, was every bit as bad. She knew very well he had been subtly interrogating Constance, and the moment the door had closed behind the other girl, she turned to him with a disapproving frown.

"There was no need for the rack and the thumbscrews, Mr. Blakely," she told him in a severe tone. "Your colleague has already questioned Constance, and all to no avail. The poor girl has naught to do with all this!"

"Thumbscrews?" Peter raised a copper eyebrow indignantly. "Truly, ma'am, you wound me. I should never resort to anything so lacking in finesse. And as for your beauteous companion not being involved, well, one never knows. Betrayal can come—"

"From anywhere," Maggie finished for him with obvious disgust. "I vow, the pair of you are as alike as two peas in a pod! Are all men so suspicious?"

"Only those of us who have learned to be," Ian said quietly. "It is the way of the world, Miss Chambers, and 'tis time you learned that fact. Your blind faith in your fellow man could well get you killed one of these days."

Maggie bristled at his condescending tones. "That might be the way of *your* world, *Sir—*" she used his abbreviated title with cutting deliberation "—but it is not the way of mine, and I thank God 'tis so! Now, if you will excuse me, I have a ball to plan, and there is much I must do. I shall leave you two cynics to your plotting, provided, of course, that you can trust each other!" And with that, she turned and stalked from the room.

It was only later, as she was poring over the lists of food Mrs. Hartcup had thoughtfully provided her, that her own words came back to trouble her. Sir Ian and Mr. Blakely were a great deal alike, she mused, brushing the plume of her quill across her cheek. Both were intelligent, incisive, with an underlying toughness that was undeniable. There was also something in their eyes that troubled her; eyes that could flirt and tease when needed, but eyes that also held a certain cold wariness.

Sir Ian said that Mr. Blakely had once been an agent of the Crown, and she could see how easily the other man could deceive others into underestimating him. But what about Sir Ian? He admitted that he was a rake traveling incognito to escape the Runners, and there was something in his hard and complicated manner that made her accept his tales of a life wasted on cards and wine.

But was that all? What other secrets did he hide behind his mask of cynicism? She gave a weary sigh and then turned her attention back to the lists spread out before her, determinedly pushing her troubled thoughts to the back of her mind.

Chapter Ten

$\mathcal{N}$ow that he had the fiction of the dinner party to keep him at Bride's Leap, Ian abandoned his pose as an invalid. The next morning he and Peter accompanied the ladies out to the stables to choose their mounts for the morning's ride. Ian stood quietly, watching in amusement as Maggie worked her charm on the ancient groom, but when the stable hand brought out a large bay stallion with a side-saddle strapped to his back, his smile soon faded.

"Good God, Miss Chambers, isn't that the black-hearted devil who ran away with you once before?" he protested, his brows gathering in an angry frown. "Surely you don't intend to ride him again!"

Maggie glanced at him in surprise. "But of course I do," she said, patting the big bay's neck with a fond hand. "Tartar and I have reached an understanding, and he is my mount now, aren't you, my brave fellow?"

As if agreeing with Maggie, the stallion nodded his head, his bridle jangling noisily. Ian, however, was not appeased, and strode forward to place a restraining hand on Maggie's arm. "You are not going to ride this animal, and that is final," he announced through gritted teeth. "Take one of the other horses."

Maggie's jaw dropped at such high-handedness. "For your information, sir, I—"

"At ease, Captain!" Peter interrupted with a light laugh. "Miss Chambers isn't one of your hussars, you know. If she wants to ride the wretched beast, let her. It is not your place to bark orders at her." And he shot Ian a warning look that silenced him.

"You are quite right, Peter," he managed when he had regained his temper. He could see Miss Spenser and the other servants were regarding him with open interest, and cursed his lack of control. Swallowing his pride, he turned to Maggie with a low bow. "Miss Chambers, pray forgive me. I hadn't meant to snap at you like that. I fear the mantle of command is not so easily discarded as I thought."

Maggie felt that this was the truest statement she had yet to hear him utter, and gave him a civil smile. "Consider yourself forgiven, Captain," she said, accepting his aid as she sprang into the saddle. "Although I suppose I shouldn't be surprised by your protests; Dr. Garlowe said much the same thing when I first rode Tartar. I only hope you won't be as preoccupied with my safety as he and Constance," she added ruefully, "else I fear I shall never be let off the leading strings!"

A few minutes later, the quartet was riding out of the stable yards and galloping across the fields towards the sea. With the adroitness learned in society as well as in battle, Peter succeeded in pairing off with Constance, leaving Maggie and Ian to follow at a discreet distance. After they had ridden a short distance, Ian was the first to speak, but rather than offering another apology as she half expected, he said, "What did you mean by that?"

"By what?" Maggie tightened her hands on the

reins, giving Tartar an admonishing taste of her spurs. The animal obviously knew he was a source of contention, and was doing his best to make mischief. It took all of Maggie's limited skills to keep him firmly in hand.

"About Miss Spenser and Dr. Garlowe being concerned for your welfare," Ian clarified, his tone thoughtful as he gave her a considering stare. "Have they been worried about you?"

"Yes, and before that suspicious little mind of yours can attach any evil intentions to them, I think I should remind you that Dr. Garlowe is a physician," Maggie said, gauging well the gleam in his dark blue eyes. "And as such, it is hardly surprising that he should concern himself with the well-being of others. As for Constance, she *is* my companion, you know."

Ian was silent as they continued their ride. "How long has she been your companion?"

"Nine . . . no, ten weeks now," Maggie answered, privately amazed at how fast time was passing. "Mr. Bigley hired her not long after I came to stay with him and his wife. I remember thinking how ludicrous that was; a companion in need of a companion. That's what I was before I inherited Great-Uncle's blunt, you know; a companion."

Ian realized he hadn't known that. In fact, there was a great deal about Miss Chambers that he did not know. Perhaps the mystery of the missing heir lay in her past, but first things first. For now, he was interested in her lovely companion.

"Then you never hired her?"

"Oh no, it was all done through Mr. Bigley's agent in London. Mr. Bigley said he'd written Bride's Leap asking that one of the other maids be sent to chaperone me, and the next thing he knew, Constance was arriving on the doorstep, a note from a London agency in her hand."

"That seems a rather convoluted way of engaging a companion," Ian answered, puzzling over her answer. "How did Mr. Bigley's London agent learn of his need if he first wrote to Bride's Leap?"

Maggie drew up her horse, turning startled gray eyes to Ian. "Do you know, I have never thought of that," she marveled. "I suppose I assumed when Hartcup couldn't find an acceptable companion here, he wrote to the agent himself."

"But you never asked?"

"Of course not."

"Good God, why?"

"Because there was no need." Maggie glowered at him. "I am perfectly content with Constance, and I certainly wouldn't presume to criticize the way Hartcup runs the household."

"But you don't even know if he is the one who hired the blasted creature!" Ian snapped, maddened by her blindness.

"Well, of course he did." The look Maggie cast him made it evident she doubted his mental acuity. "How else would she have learned of the position?"

Ian opened his lips to utter a blistering setdown, when he suddenly closed his mouth again. "How else indeed," he echoed, his heart beginning to race with familiar excitement.

Maggie shot him a suspicious look, not at all sure she cared for the remote look on his handsome face. She was beginning to recognize that expression; it meant he was plotting something.

They continued their ride in silence until they were rejoined by Constance and Peter. The other man was looking particularly smug, and Maggie had the strong suspicion he had been questioning Constance again. She glanced at her companion curiously, and for the first time, she felt a niggling doubt. In the next moment she was filled with horrified remorse, ashamed of herself for her lack of faith.

Of course Constance was innocent of any wrongdoing, she told herself, listening with half an ear as Mr. Blakely extolled the virtues of the Cornish countryside. Only look at how upset she had been the night of the attack, and since then, she had been as devoted and concerned as a sister. No, she shook her head firmly. She refused to even entertain the possibility that Constance was involved in any of this.

"Then you do not agree?" Peter was looking at her in surprise. "I made certain you would, considering the events of the past few days."

Maggie blinked at him in surprise, a warm flush of embarrassment stealing across her face at the realization she'd been caught wool-gathering. "I'm very sorry, Mr. Blakely, I fear I wasn't attending. What was it you were saying?"

"What? Do you mean to say you weren't hanging on to my every word?" the redheaded man protested with a boyish pout. "Really, ma'am, you must have care for my reputation as a raconteur! I shall be quite ruined if it is bandied about that my listeners are nodding off in the middle of my witticisms."

Maggie smiled at him. "Were you uttering any?"

"A hit, Miss Chambers, a palpable hit!" he cried, clutching his hand to the front of his brown velvet riding jacket. "But as it happens, I was speaking of the scenery hereabouts, and how well it would fit into one of those dreadful Minervian novels you ladies so cherish. Do you not agree?"

"As I have read but a few of those books, Mr. Blakely, I hardly think it can be said that I cherish them." Maggie felt honor-bound to defend herself from the dandy's teasing attack. "But you might consult Captain Sherrill," she said, shooting Ian a wicked smile. "He has confessed to actually having read one. Is that not so, sir?"

"You, Marcus?" Peter looked genuinely shocked. "Never say 'tis true!"

Ian squirmed in his saddle, uncomfortable at being the center of so much attention. "When one is shot and laid up for weeks at a time, one will read almost anything," he said, defending his choice of literature with a grumble. "And for your information, Peter, I quite agree with you; Bride's Leap is the perfect setting for a gothic. A fact that has already been proven to an alarming degree; as I have told you."

"Yes, and I think it horribly unfair of you all to have deprived me of the fun," Peter put in with another pout. "Really, Miss Chambers, if you count yourself any sort of hostess at all, you will hold another ghost hunt *tout de suite*. One of my ancestors was Irish, although my mother denies it most emphatically, and I daresay that if anyone could sniff out a ghost, it would be I."

Maggie remembered the unpleasant result of the last ghost hunt, and was about to put her foot firmly down when she caught Sir Ian's eye. He gave an almost imperceptible nod of his head, and she realized that he wanted her to agree. Without pausing to weigh the matter, she did just that.

"As I am in hopes of establishing myself as a hostess extraordinaire, Mr. Blakely, you shall have your ghost hunt," she said, inclining her head with a gracious smile. "But you and the captain may search the cellars yourself. Constance and I shall stay in the parlor this time, won't we, my dear?" She shot Constance a quick smile.

"Indeed we shall, Miss Chambers." Constance shuddered delicately. "I quite get the vapors when I think of you locked in that dreadful little wine

147

cellar with no possible way out. How fortunate the good captain was able to rescue you yet again."

By the time they reached the main house, Peter was in a fever to begin ghost-hunting, and without even pausing to change their clothes, he and Ian went directly down to the cellars. "I trust there is a reason for this charade," Ian grumbled, holding the torch in his hand as the two walked towards the wine cellar. "You know full well there isn't a drop of the Irish in you."

"Perhaps, but with this red hair and my glib tongue, the explanation has oft stood me in good stead," Peter replied roguishly. "But as for the rest of it, I do have a very good reason for dragging you down here. I think I may be on to something."

"What?" Ian was instantly all business. "Did Miss Spenser let anything slip?"

"Heavens no, that one is as sweet as lilacs in May," Peter replied, running his hand over the damp stone next to the stairway. "She can talk and sigh all morning long, and never reveal a single thing; if she were a man, I'd swear she was hiding something."

"Then why this sudden preoccupation with ghosts? And what the devil is it you are looking for?"

"Because while Miss Spenser and I were riding ahead of you, I happened to catch a glimpse of Bride's Leap, and looking at it put me strongly in mind of the old house not far from my father's estate in Kent. And thinking of that put me strongly in mind of . . . this." He pressed the corner of one of the stones, and to Ian's amazement, the whole wall suddenly swung open, revealing a black cavity hidden in the stony surface.

"My God," he exclaimed, holding his torch in front of him as he cautiously stepped inside. "A secret passage! This whole thing is beginning to get more and more like a bloody gothic with each passing day! How far does it go?"

"Well, we'll never find out standing here and gawking at it," Peter said, pulling a small pistol from the waistband of his riding breeches. At Ian's stare, he gave a negligent shrug. "Marchfield told me you preferred your agents armed."

Ian grinned at the younger man, retrieving from his pocket a knife Samuel had smuggled him. "So I do, Blakely," he said, switching the torch from his right hand to his left. "Let's go."

The passage, while dusty and narrow, wended its way from the very bottom of the cellars to the upper reaches of the servants' quarters, and Ian noted grimly that it appeared to have been used rather recently. Most of the entryways into the passage had been closed decades ago, while others were freshly oiled and swung open at the slightest touch. When the third door he tried on the second floor opened in this fashion, Ian and Peter found themselves standing outside on a stone balcony.

"Watch your step," Ian cautioned, drawing Peter carefully back inside. "Unless I'm much mistaken, this is the balcony just outside Miss Chambers's room, and we have been warned that it is about to collapse."

"I can see that," Peter replied, indicating the cracked and crumbling masonry with a finger. "It's a wonder it hasn't given way already. Why the devil does she continue sleeping in there if it's so dangerous?"

"Why does that blasted female do anything?" Ian retorted with a grumble, carefully closing the secret door and resuming his search of the passageway. "Because she is a stubborn, willful hoyden who would rather die than do the sensible thing! Doubtlessly someone told her she couldn't stay in the room, and that is all it took to make her barricade herself inside."

"Yes, I noted how well she takes to gentle handling." Peter gave Ian a wicked look. "For shame, Sir, and here I was certain your reputation as a rake was well earned! Do you mean to say you cannot control one little spinster?"

Ian felt an odd sense of unreality. He had had almost this very same conversation with Marchfield while the duke was investigating the notorious Lady X. That Lady X was revealed to be Jacinda Malvern, whom the duke later married, was purely coincidental, but Ian remembered taking Anthony to task for failing to use his charm to coerce her into cooperating. Not that he had any intention of marrying Miss Chambers, or any other female, for that matter, but—

"Look out!" The warning came almost a moment too late, as Ian realized he was about to walk down a flight of stairs he hadn't even seen until Peter pulled him back.

"Where the hell did these come from?" he asked, bending down to run a hand over the top step's dusty and uneven surface. "Unless we have been walking in circles, isn't the staircase in the north wing of the house?"

"Umm, and we are in the west wing, facing the ocean," Peter agreed, bending down to see what Ian was examining. When the flame of his torch flickered and almost died, Ian straightened at once.

"There's a breeze blowing," he said, his fingers tightening on the handle of his knife. "There must be a door to the outside somewhere nearby; shall we see if we can find it?"

"If we must." Peter looked uncertain. "The balcony isn't the only thing that looks in imminent danger of collapsing. Are you sure you want to risk it?"

Ian's rakish grin was answer enough, and Peter followed him down the staircase, muttering all the while about spy-masters with more bottom than brains. The stairs led to another corridor, and the farther along the corridor they traveled, the more they became aware of the smell and the sound of the sea. Some ten minutes later, they found themselves outside, staring at a crumbled stone wall with interest.

"Damn." Ian's voice was harsh as he realized the implications of his discovery.

"My sentiments exactly, Sir," Peter said, the expression on his face growing increasingly grim as he glanced about him. "There's little we can do to protect Miss Chambers if our villain has complete access to the house any time he chooses to use it. And we dare not close the passage without tipping our hand. What are you going to do?"

"I haven't decided just yet," Ian admitted, turning various possibilities over in his mind as he walked to the wall. "But I think we can start by laying a few traps in the passage; nothing fatal, mind you, but enough to let us know when the passage has been used."

"That might be advisable," Peter said, grimacing as his feet sunk lower in the thick mud that surrounded the wall. "The passage's existence would hardly be known to outsiders, which indicates our friend must have a confederate in the household. From what I have gathered, most of the servants have been employed here since Adam was in knee britches, and any of them could easily be involved."

"Perhaps—" Ian's voice was distant "—but as it happens, the person I have in mind is a more recent addition to the staff. Blakely, do you still have that friend in London?"

"I have many friends," Peter answered, realizing Sir was asking about an informant, "and I suppose

151

I should write to let him know I have arrived safely. Is there a message you should like to send? I am sure he would be more than happy to see that it is delivered."

"That is very thoughtful of you, Blakely." Ian shot him a bland smile. "I would like your friend to contact a certain agent for me and see where he hires his servants."

"Looking for a majordomo, are you?"

Ian's eyes took on a cold gleam. "No, but I am most interested in acquiring a companion."

"Thank you, Mrs. Hartcup," Maggie said as she accepted the list of neighbors from the house-keeper. "I don't know what I should have done without your assistance."

"Oh, 'tis my pleasure, miss," the older woman replied, her cheeks pinking with excitement. "And may I say how much we're all looking forward to this party? Why, we've not had so much as an af-ternoon tea here since the old gentleman took sick, and before that, well, the kind of entertainments he enjoyed weren't the kind of things I ought to be discussing with a young lady like you."

"Really?" A vague memory stirred in Maggie's brain, something her grandfather had once said about her great-uncle's rakish ways, but she couldn't quite remember what he had said. Oh well, she supposed it didn't signify, and turned her at-tention back to the list. She paused at one name that had a question mark beside it.

"Mrs. Hartcup, who are the Varney's?"

"Oh, they be the local squire and his lady," Mrs. Hartcup replied, looking vastly uncomfortable. "I included them because it wouldn't do to leave them off, but I'd not count on them attending if I was you."

"Whyever not?" Maggie asked, frowning at the possibility of her gentry neighbors snubbing her.

"Well, miss, 'tis because of the scandal, I suppose."

"The ghost, do you mean?" Maggie asked, genuinely perplexed. "Surely they can't hold that against me! Heavens, it happened over a hundred years ago!"

"Not that scandal, 'tis the other one, involving your great-uncle and their governess," Mrs. Hartcup explained, leaning forward in her chair in a confiding manner. "He ruined her, you know."

"He did?" Maggie was torn between shock and avid interest. It was human nature, she decided ruefully; everyone enjoyed hearing of another's downfall.

"It was all kept very hushed, you understand," Mrs. Hartcup continued eagerly. "But it seems the old gentleman was meeting her on the sly, and well, nature being what it is, they was soon found out, and the squire demanded that he make amends and marry the poor girl."

"As Uncle Ellsworth died without heirs, I take it he refused?"

"Aye, that he did, miss, and in a most brutal manner, too. Said he'd not be giving his name to 'soiled goods,' and him the one that did the soiling!" The housekeeper gave a disgusted snort. "But that's the way of the world, isn't it? The gentlemen take their pleasure, and 'tis left to the poor girl to pay the piper."

"Whatever became of her?" Maggie asked, feeling a wave of pity for the hapless governess. "Did she have the babe?"

"No one ever knew. She just disappeared one night and never came back. Some say she went to Surrey, where she had family, while others say she

153

took the only course open to a female in her circumstance."

Maggie sat back, a sudden excitement beginning to build in her as she realized the import of Mrs. Hartcup's story. Sir Ian said there was doubtlessly an illegitimate heir somewhere about, and that he was probably the one responsible for the attacks on her. Feigning an indifference she was far from feeling, she leaned back in her chair.

"What was the poor woman's name, Mrs. Hartcup? Did anyone ever tell you?"

"Oh, there was no need for anyone to be telling me anything, miss." The housekeeper bristled with indignation. "I was right here when it all happened, and I remember the shame of it well!"

"But what was her name?" Maggie pressed.

"Jessica, miss. Jessica Clayburt."

Chapter Eleven

"Clayburt?" Maggie echoed, wondering why the name sounded so familiar to her.

"Aye, miss, and she was a taking little thing, with the prettiest brown eyes you ever did see," Mrs. Hartcup said with a reminiscent sigh. "The scandal of it was the talk of the neighborhood for months! I often thought the old man's illness was a judgment from God . . . if you don't mind my saying so."

"Indeed not, Mrs. Hartcup," Maggie assured her, horrified that one of her ancestors could have treated another human being so cavalierly. "In fact, I hope the old goat is roasting in a particularly choice piece of hell!" As her indignation faded, she considered what other information Sir Ian would need to help him in his quest.

"Er . . . how long ago was all this, Mrs. Hartcup?" she asked innocently. "It must have been while he was in his youth. I recall Grandpapa saying he was a dreadful roué."

"No, miss, he was all of fifty when it happened,

and poor Miss Clayburt was scarce five and twenty!"

Maggie did some swift calculations. She knew her great-uncle died a month before his eighty-first birthday, which would mean that if there was a child, he would be thirty years old. She tucked the information away, along with the governess's name, feeling smugly pleased by her cleverness. She couldn't wait to see Sir Ian's face when she told him.

Upon leaving her study, she went in search of him and was mildly annoyed to learn he and Mr. Blakely had ridden into town. "Did he say when they would be returning?" she asked Hartcup, striving to swallow her disappointment.

"No, Miss Chambers," the butler replied, studying her with interest. "The captain did, however, request that I give you a message."

"What is it?" she asked, hoping for some word of where he had gone. Perhaps they were at the inn, and she and Constance could ride into town and join them. She'd only been in the tiny village a few times since her arrival, and—

"Stay put."

"I beg your pardon?" Maggie said, blinking at Hartcup's clipped command.

"Those were Captain Sherrill's instructions, miss." Although the butler's face was set in its usual impassive lines, Maggie had the impression he was smirking at her. "I believe his exact words were 'Tell the little minx she is to stay put, and that I'll be back when I can.'"

"I see," Maggie replied, her teeth clenching at Sir Ian's audacity. "Was there anything else?"

"No, Miss Chambers, although he did say he would probably be gone for luncheon."

Maggie thanked him tersely and went back to her study. She was toying with the notion of flaunting his orders when her good sense came to the fore. Autocratic though he might be, Sir Ian only had her safety in mind, and it would be foolish beyond all permission to disobey him out of spite. Besides, she admitted with a rueful sigh, where would she go?

She spent the rest of the morning putting the finishing touches to the menu and drawing up the guest list for the dinner party. She included the Varneys, hoping they would come, and also added Mr. Bigley to the list. The older man and his rather vague wife had been kindness itself to her while she was a guest in their home, and she was anxious to return their hospitality.

It was just as she was finishing the last of her lists that she heard a commotion in the hallway, and a few seconds later, the door to her study was thrown open. Miss Thomas stood there, her sallow complexion flushed with triumph. "We are returned, Miss Chambers," she announced dramatically, sailing into the room to stand before Maggie's desk. "Have there been any more visitations?"

"None that I am aware of," Maggie replied, setting her pen down with a sigh. She had resigned herself to the other woman's presence, and in fact, was rather grateful for it. Now that she had two gentlemen residing under her roof, she knew some kind of chaperone was required if she didn't wish to put herself beyond the pale.

"Well, perhaps our luck will change," Leonora said, picking up a list from the desk and scanning it without bothering to ask Maggie's permission. "What is this?" she asked, her dark brows meeting in a frown. "Surely you don't mean to invite all these people to our séance? It will never do, you know. Such affairs are best kept to as small a number as possible, so as not to frighten the ghost."

Frightening ghosts seemed a contradiction in

terms to Maggie, but she managed not to smile. "That is the list for my dinner party," she managed with equanimity. "And as for the séance, I am not at all sure it is such a good idea. We—"

"But Robert has his heart set on this," Leonora protested. "He has been studying, and I am certain he will be more than successful in ridding your home of this unclean spirit."

"Well, perhaps after the dinner party." Maggie decided it might be advisable to let the matter pass for the moment. "I will discuss this with Captain Sherrill, and—"

"Yes, I had heard that he was still here, and that his friend, a rather ramshackle fellow, from all accounts, has joined him," Miss Thomas said, her lips thinning in annoyance. "Really, Miss Chambers, are you quite sure that is proper?"

"Considering that both are *invited* guests, I should think so." Maggie was unable to resist the subtle dig at Leonora. "Besides, now that you and your sainted brother are here, I am sure that even the most prudish of souls will be appeased. No one could dare attach any impropriety to either of your names." And she shot her a poisonous smile.

Leonora bristled at the very thought. "I should like to see someone try!" she said, her black eyes dancing with fire. "Never fear, Miss Chambers, with Robert and me here, your good reputation is guaranteed!"

It was approaching four before Ian and Peter returned to Bride's Leap. They had spent an exhausting day at the inn, drinking inferior ale and listening to local gossip. They had also made contact with another of Peter's "friends," and a set of messages and instructions was already on its way to London.

"I hope you are right about this Shaye fellow,"

he told Peter as they made their way back to the house from the stables. "He had a rather shifty aspect to him."

"All part of his charm, Sir, I assure you," Peter said with a cheeky grin. "How else could he move about London's underworld so successfully? An honest, upright-looking man would be distrusted on sight. Besides, he is loyal to me, and I would trust him with my life."

Ian thought of the large, unkempt man with the scar running across his cheek and wondered how Peter could be so trusting. Hadn't he learned yet that a spy could rely on no one; not even the woman he loved?

As if in answer to his unspoken thoughts, Peter said, "I know that you have a reputation for wariness, Sir, and I daresay you have cause, but that is not the way I choose to live either my personal or professional life. To exist is to take a chance, and I suppose that is the way I prefer things."

Ian heard and accepted the implied criticism of the guarded manner in which he conducted himself. Once he had regarded such caution as inevitable, but now he was beginning to wonder. Had he grown too cold; too secretive; holding at a distance the very people who might one day help him?

The thought was a depressing one, as was the thought of what would happen once peace came. Naturally there would always be a need for a man with his unique abilities; espionage was an accepted part of international politics. But as the need for his services grew less acute, what would his life be like?

"I didn't mean to insult you, Sir," Peter said, shooting Ian an anxious look. "I just wanted to let you know that you can rely on Shaye; just as I hope you rely on me."

Ian shook off his melancholy and shot Peter a smile. "I do rely on you, Blakely, very much so, and I suppose I also trust your large friend. It is just my nature to be cautious; I trust I haven't given offense."

If Peter was surprised by Ian's apology, he was careful to hide it. Instead he gave a wicked laugh. "Good Gad, Sir, after some of the snubs and set-downs I have been given, you needn't worry about offending my sensibilities! In fact, I sincerely doubt that I even possess any, and I must say I am the better for it. Such pesky things, sensibilities."

Maggie was waiting in the hallway when they walked through the door, and they'd barely had time to hand their hats and gloves to Hartcup before she was on them. "Where the devil have you been?" she demanded, casting a furtive glance over her shoulder. "Our guests are here and driving me mad!"

"Didn't you get my message?" Ian asked, hiding his amusement at her obvious agitation.

"Oh yes, and you will be happy to know that I 'stayed put' just as you ordered." Her eyes flashed with temper. "But that doesn't answer my question! The Thomases have been here a donkey's age, and it has been left to me to entertain them. They are upstairs now dressing for tea, and—"

"What do you mean, it has been left to you?" Ian interrupted her tirade. "Where is Miss Spenser?"

"How am I to know?" she exclaimed, her hands on her hips. "I don't keep the poor girl on a leash, you know; she is entitled to some time off."

"When will you be serving tea?" Ian asked, disregarding the last part of her statement.

"In about thirty minutes, but I suppose I can set it back another thirty minutes so that you and Mr. Blakely can change." She raised an eyebrow at their rather disheveled appearance.

"Do that," Ian instructed, starting for the stairs with Peter hot on his heels, "but meet me in the library in forty minutes. There is something I need to tell you."

"But—"

"Forty minutes." And then he was gone, leaving Maggie standing at the bottom of the stairs with an aggrieved scowl on her face.

Maggie was in the library at the appointed time and was pacing the room when Ian made his appearance. He was dressed in a jacket of blue Bath superfine and a pair of cream-colored trousers, his blond hair combed to ruthless perfection. Not wishing to be caught admiring him, Maggie took her chair beside the fireplace and shot him a cool look. "Well?" she asked imperiously. "What is it you wanted to say?"

Ian's eyes gleamed in appreciation of her fiery temperament. She was wearing a new gown of amber silk trimmed with gold lace, and with her coppery hair wound in a coronet, she looked as regal as a goddess. "I heard some rather interesting gossip in the village about your great-uncle," he said, crossing one foot over the other. "It seems he had something of a reputation where the ladies were concerned. The possibility of there being an illegitimate heir seems to be increasing, and with a little time, I should know his name."

"I think you should start with a woman named Jessica Clayburt," Maggie said, taking a perverse pleasure in stealing some of his thunder. He sounded so pompous and in command that it quite set her teeth on edge. "She was said to be carrying Uncle Ellsworth's child when she disappeared."

"What?" Ian sat forward, his brows snapping together. "What are you talking about?"

"Why, Uncle's affair with the Varneys' governess," Maggie said in a sweet tone, fluttering her lashes at him. "It was all the talk of the neighborhood some thirty years ago. Don't tell me you didn't know."

He ignored her jibe. "What was the name again?"

"Clayburt; at least that is what Mrs. Hartcup told

161

me," Maggie replied, forgetting her anger in her eagerness to impart what she had learned. "I must own the name sounds familiar, although I cannot place it. But at least now we have a place to start; which is more than we had before."

"Mmm," Ian agreed, rubbing his cheek thoughtfully. "Were you able to learn anything else?" he asked.

"Miss Clayburt apparently had family in Surrey, and that is where she was said to have gone," Maggie said, her excitement fading in light of his indifference. She thought her news would have rated some show of interest, however small, and she found his lack of response annoying. "Did you and Mr. Blakely find anything when you went ghost-hunting?" she demanded, shooting him a challenging look.

"No," Ian replied truthfully, his mouth quirking in a wry smile. "Peter was most incensed; he claims this ghost business is all a hum."

Maggie smiled as she imagined the other man's boyish pout. "He'd be singing a different tune if he'd actually seen her," she replied, her gray eyes growing dark at the memory of the mind-stopping terror she'd felt at the sight of the ethereal figure standing in the moonlight.

Ian studied her pensive expression. "But did you really see a ghost?" he asked, ignoring the sudden impulse he felt to reach out and touch the fiery brightness of her hair. "We've never talked about what happened that night, and I think it's time we did; now, before the others join us. I want you to tell me everything that you saw."

Maggie complied, adding more detail now that she didn't fear his ridicule. When she finished, he was frowning. "You say the door to your balcony was open?"

"Yes, and yet the next morning when I examined it, it was locked just as it had always been. I thought perhaps it was just a dream because I was sleeping so heavily, but it seemed so terribly real."

Ian stiffened at her words. "You were sleeping heavier than usual?"

She nodded. "I know warm milk is said to have a soporific effect, but really, it was the strangest thing. I remember lying there, and it was as if I couldn't move, or even think. Everything seemed so hazy, so unreal, as if—"

"As if you were drugged," Ian concluded, his voice harsh. "Which I strongly suspect you were."

"Drugged!" Maggie's stomach plunged to the toes of her slippers. "But that is nonsense! Constance prepared the milk for me herself, and . . ." Her voice trailed off as her eyes widened in comprehension.

"No," she whispered, shaking her head violently, "no, I refuse to consider it for even one moment! Constance is my friend; she'd never betray me!"

Ian's heart ached for her obvious pain. He recognized the shattered look in her eyes, for it had been in his own eyes as he watched Lynette walking away, leaving him in the hands of the French dragoons. He moved from his chair to kneel before her, his hands warm and comforting as they closed about hers.

"It's only speculation," he said gently, his breath stirring the cluster of curls at her temple. "We have no proof that links her to the inheritance or the attacks on you, but I think it is a possibility you should consider."

"You think it likely," Maggie said, her own hand coming up to cup his firm jaw. She felt more alone than she had ever felt in her entire life, and she needed the reassurance of a human touch.

"I think it likely," he agreed, staring down at her moist lips. They looked so soft, so vulnerable, and without thinking, he bent his head and placed a gentle kiss against them. His only intent had been to comfort her, but the feel of her warm mouth beneath his destroyed that fiction, and he was soon kissing her with the fierce passion he had been denying since the first moment he saw her.

Maggie felt his passion, and answered it with her own shy desire. Ian was the only comfort in a world suddenly fraught with danger, and she clung to him with a strength born of desperation.

"Maggie." He whispered her name in urgent tones, his mouth moving down the slender column of her neck to where her pulse was beating wildly. All the lectures he had given his agents over the years about the dangers of becoming involved while on a mission flew from his head, and for the first time in more than a decade, he allowed his emotions free rein.

The rattling of the doorknob was their only warning, and they'd barely had time to break apart before the door opened and Peter and Constance came into the room. Ian leapt to his feet, turning quickly to face the fireplace, seeking to hide the urgent proof of the unslaked desire that was thundering through his veins. His hands clenched into tight fists as he fought to control himself, and it was some seconds before he felt it safe to turn and face the others.

"Good afternoon, Miss Spenser," he said, his voice carefully controlled as he bowed to her. "I trust you have had a pleasant afternoon?"

"Oh yes, Captain Sherrill," she replied, her smile sweet as she studied him. "I spent a lovely afternoon walking by the cliffs. Which reminds me, Miss Chambers." Her blue eyes flashed to Maggie's flushed face. "I happened to see Dr. Garlowe on my way back, and I invited him to tea. I hope you don't mind?"

"No, of course not, Constance," she replied, praying her inner trepidation didn't show. She felt as if she were in a whirlwind; cast down so low one moment, and then swept up to the heavens in the next. She stole a surreptitious look at Ian's hard face, and knew a vague disappointment that he could appear so cool

164

and unconcerned. Had their embrace meant so little to him? she wondered, and then his eyes met hers, and in their flaming blue depths, she read her answer.

The Thomases soon joined them, and as usual, Leonora dominated the conversation. Dr. Garlowe arrived while she was treating them to Robert's theory as to the best way of disposing of the ghost, and Maggie used his appearance to change the conversation.

"I was wondering if you have had a chance to see more of the area, Doctor," she said, flashing him an encouraging smile. "I believe you said that, like me, you are a newcomer here?"

"A relative newcomer." His lips quirked in a smile. "But then, to the Cornish, anyone whose family hasn't been here for at least four generations is an alien invader and suspect. You are lucky your family has been at Bride's Leap for so long, ma'am, else you would find yourself as much of an outsider as I. It is very heard to treat people who regard you with such suspicion."

Maggie could sympathize with his plight, but then she realized what he had said and she frowned at him. "But I thought you said your mother's family was from the area," she told him, unaware of the way Ian stiffened with sudden interest. "Surely that should give you some credence with the locals."

"That's because you don't know the Cornish." Dr. Garlowe was smiling at her. "And a few summers spent with distant relations hardly qualifies one as a bona fide resident. But I pray you pay me no mind. I spent a rather unprofitable afternoon trying to convince a local fisherman who is suffering from a lung complaint to try my tonic rather than the gypsy brew he swears by, and he'd have none of it."

"Perhaps if you put as much brandy in your tonic as the gypsy uses in hers, you might have better success," Peter volunteered, his bright blue eyes resting on the doctor.

"That is so," Dr. Garlowe admitted ruefully. "Old Mr. Bressan did reek of spirits, now that you mention it."

The conversation saw them safely through the rest of the hour, and all too soon, Dr. Garlowe was rising to his feet. "Thank you so much for your kind hospitality, Miss Chambers," he said, smiling as he took her hand. "I hope we might do this again sometime."

"As do I." Maggie could feel Ian's eyes on her and wondered what she had done to put that hard look on his face. "I am holding a small dinner party next week to thank Captain Sherrill, and I would like it very much if you were to attend. I'll be mailing the invitations at the end of the week, but I wanted to ask you in person."

"That is very kind of you, Miss Chambers; thank you." He looked genuinely flattered at her invitation. "Meanwhile, I was wondering if you would care to join me when I call on one of my patients. She is rather elderly and somewhat set in her ways, and I know she would welcome your presence."

"I'm afraid that's impossible," Ian began automatically, only to be interrupted by Maggie.

"I should be delighted, Dr. Garlowe; thank you." Maggie sent Ian a quelling look. "I've only met but a few of my neighbors; shall we say tomorrow morning at ten?"

Dr. Garlowe agreed readily to the hour and soon departed, leaving an uncomfortable silence in his wake. Maggie was aware of Ian's disapproval, but her only response was to inch her chin higher and cast him a defiant look. She knew her behavior was childish, but she simply didn't care.

Her emotions were extremely volatile at the moment, and the power of them left her confused and strangely vulnerable. She wanted nothing more than to go off somewhere by herself and examine these strange new feelings, but there were her guests to think of. Swallowing her disappointment, she resumed her seat, listening half-attentively to Constance and Peter's discussion of the latest London scandal. Although she laughed and smiled in what she hoped was an appropriate manner, she was remembering those magical moments when Ian had taken her in his arms. How could she have behaved so wantonly?

That was much the same question she was asking herself later that night as she sat before her mirror. She thought she looked just the same, although it seemed her lips held an inviting redness that wasn't there before. She touched them tentatively, her eyes closing as she remembered the way they had softened beneath Ian's hard mouth.

It wasn't the first time a man had kissed her, but it was the first time she had kissed back, wanting things that she now blushed to think of. Heaven only knew what Ian felt about her behavior, she thought, covering her face with a low groan. Perhaps that is why he objected to her driving out with Dr. Garlowe. Not because he was jealous, but because he feared she would do something to disgrace them all.

She dropped her hands to her lap and opened her eyes, her expression bleak as she regarded her reflection. How had her life grown so terribly complicated? she wondered with an unhappy sigh. Less than a year ago, her only concern was trying to live another day without throttling Mrs. Graft; now look at her. She had a fortune that could well get her killed, a companion she wasn't all that sure she could trust, and a vengeful ghost haunting her nights. And as if all that weren't bad enough, she feared she'd done one thing more foolish than all the rest. She had fallen in love with Sir Ian Charles.

Chapter Twelve

𝔐aggie wasn't the only one to suffer pangs of regret. Ian spent most of that night lying in bed and cursing his own lack of control. He, better than any man, knew the dangers of mixing emotions and business while on a mission, and yet he had been unable to help himself. Maggie had felt so good in his arms, so right, and he had been swept away on a wave of raw desire unlike any he had ever felt before.

Perhaps the prince had been right to make him take this leave of absence, he mused, shifting restlessly onto his back and staring up at the ceiling. In his present state, his mind was much too befuddled to be of any use to the Crown. He smiled bitterly at the thought of all that had transpired in the sennight since he had set out from Marchfield's. He had fought off an assailant, been in a carriage accident, and was now involved in a mystery that sounded as if it had been lifted from the pages of a book. Somehow he doubted that this was what His Highness had in mind when he ordered him on holiday.

Just as swiftly as it came, his smile vanished. What was he going to do? Even if he were simply Sir Ian Charles, rake and ne'er-do-well, the feelings he bore for Maggie would still be untenable. She was an heiress, the owner of a beautiful mansion, while he barely clung to the skirts of respectability. There was money, of course, but nothing approaching the fortune she controlled, and his reputation was such that he would do her no honor in offering her his name. But he was more than Sir Ian Charles.

As "Sir," he lived a dangerous and deadly existence, courting death on a daily basis. He had spent the last ten years of his life with that inevitability and he accepted it, just as he accepted the fact that sometimes he had to kill in order to survive. His world was cold and harsh, and he could see no way of including a wife within its icy bounds.

Dr. Garlowe was waiting with his curricle when Maggie came out to the stables the next morning. She'd slept little the night before, and knew her face reflected the fact, but she was too heartsick to care. After bidding the doctor a subdued good morning, she accepted his hand into the carriage, and they were soon on their way. They hadn't gone very far when he turned to her, his brown eyes taking in her pale appearance with obvious concern.

"Are you feeling all right, Miss Chambers?" he asked, his tone kind as he studied her. "You will forgive me for being so ungentlemanly, but you are looking rather wan."

She summoned up a smile for his benefit. "You couldn't be ungentlemanly if you tried, Doctor," she told him, infusing her voice with warmth. "It is just that I didn't sleep very well last night, and I'm feeling rather fagged; that is all."

"Then perhaps it would have been better if you'd

stayed home this morning," he said, his brows knitting with worry. "You could have left a note with the butler; I would have understood."

"Oh no, it's nothing as serious as all that." She roused herself enough to smile brightly. "Besides, a carriage ride in the brisk sea air is just what I need to blow the cobwebs from my mind."

"Was it the ghost?"

It took a few moments for his question to sink in, and when it did, she gave a light laugh. "No, nothing so dramatic, I fear. Although it would have been no small wonder if I had dreamed of the ghost. Miss Thomas prattled on about it all evening until I was praying the creature would appear, and carry Miss Thomas off with her when she departed. Although I am sure I should not be saying so." And her eyes danced with laughter.

Dr. Garlowe gave a slight smile, in response. "Where were the good captain and his friend, if I may ask? I heard they spent most of yesterday at the village inn; did they go back out, do you know?"

His question startled Maggie, and she cast him a surprised look. "Not that I am aware of, Doctor," she said, choosing her words carefully. "May I ask what business it is of yours?"

He flushed at her words, but his voice was resolute as he said, "I've been doing some discreet checking on the captain, and I fear I have some rather shocking news for you. His name isn't Captain Marcus Sherrill; it's Sir Ian Charles."

Maggie almost fell off her seat in shock. Although Ian admitted he hadn't taken any great pains in hiding his identity—other than assuming a fictitious name—she hadn't expected that he would be found out so quickly, and by a man who had already expressed doubts about his character. She wondered how best to handle the situation, and then decided that studied indifference might be her safest bet. If she acted unconcerned about his true identity, perhaps she could persuade the doctor to hold his tongue. Adopting a somewhat haughty look, she turned to Dr. Garlowe.

"I know."

"You *know*?" He was clearly stunned by her revelation.

"Of course," she replied, her brows arching over her eyes in a perfect imitation of Mrs. Graft setting an inopportune tradesman in his place. "He told me soon after the accident."

"But . . . but why did you not say something?" he demanded, running a hand through his dark hair. "Good heavens, ma'am, his reputation is the worst in England!"

"Which is precisely why I said nothing," she answered in a superior manner. "I have no desire to be gossiped about."

"But that is precisely what will happen once it becomes known you have allowed that . . . that libertine to stay under your roof!"

"Dr. Garlowe, I think you will agree that whoever the captain may or may not be, he did save my life," Maggie interrupted, fixing him with a regal stare. "I owe him much, and I refuse to set that obligation aside merely because of petty morality. I admit the situation is . . . awkward, but so long as we keep our tongues silent, no one need ever know. I trust I have made myself quite clear?"

His high color grew even more pronounced. "I hope you know that you may count upon my discretion," he muttered, his hands tightening on the reins. "But I also hope that you realize the longer he remains under your roof, the greater the chance this charade will be uncovered, and when it is, I fear for your reputation."

"You needn't worry, sir," Maggie told him coolly. "Sir Ian has told me that he will be leaving the day after the dinner party, and after that, it is doubtful we shall meet again. I trust that sets your mind at ease?"

"It does." Dr. Garlowe's voice was subdued. "And your forgiveness, Miss Chambers, if I've offended you. I only meant to warn you."

Maggie felt a twinge of guilt that she had behaved so rudely, but she told herself it was for a good cause. Sir Ian's true identity must be kept secret at all costs; not only for her benefit, but for his as well. If the Runners were after him and learned of his location . . .

"We must go back!" she cried suddenly, clapping her hand on the doctor's arm. "Turn around at once and take me back to Bride's Leap!"

"But what of our ride?" He cast her a confused look. "Have I offended you that badly?"

"No, not at all," she assured him, aflame with anxiety to warn Ian of the danger. "But I really am feeling exhausted, and would rather be taken home. Please, Doctor."

Ever the gentleman, Dr. Garlowe quickly complied, and they were soon back at Bride's Leap. Maggie paused barely long enough to thank the doctor, and then she picked up her skirts and ran into the house.

She learned from Hartcup that Ian and Mr. Blakely were in the breakfast room, and burst into the room, her heart pounding in her chest as she cried, "Ian! Ian, you have to leave right away! He knows!"

Ian leapt to his feet at Maggie's dramatic entrance, reaching automatically for the pistol tucked in his pocket. When he saw she was in no apparent danger, he returned the weapon to its hiding place. "Who knows?" he asked, crossing the room to stand before her, his hands gently cupping her shoulders. "What are you talking about?"

"Dr. Garlowe; I . . . I've just returned from our ride, and oh, Ian, he knows everything!" she gasped, tilting her head up and gazing at his with distressed eyes. "I fear he may have already told the Runners."

Ian's jaw tightened ominously. "What did he say?"

"That you're really Sir Ian Charles," she replied, drawing a steadying breath. "And that you're a—a rake."

"And what was your response?" he pressed, absorbing the implications of Maggie's words.

"I told him that I already knew. I thought that if I acted unconcerned, he would let the matter drop."

"A brilliant piece of deduction, Miss Chambers," Peter approved, his blue eyes flicking towards Ian. "Perhaps I should write London about the good doctor. It seems he has some intriguing sources of his own."

Ian gave a brief nod, grateful for Blakely's quick assessment of the situation. "What do you know of Dr. Garlowe?" he asked, turning his attention to Maggie. His hands were still resting on her shoulders, and he could think of no reason why he should remove them. "Where does he come from?"

"Surrey," she replied, all but dancing from one foot to the other in her agitation. How could he be so blasted calm when even now the Runners could be closing in on him? she wondered, a niggling suspicion forming in her mind.

"Has he ever served in the military?" Ian pressed, deciding that was the most likely place for the truth to have leaked out.

"How am I to know?" Maggie was strongly tempted to aim a well-placed kick at his shin. "He told me only that he hailed from Surrey and that he practiced in Devonshire prior to coming here.

Oh, what does that matter? Didn't you hear what I said? The Runners—"

"The Runners, Miss Chambers, are the least of our problems," Peter interrupted, exchanging a hard glance with Ian as he rose to his feet. "I'll ride into the village. If he's used any of the usual sources, I should have my answer within an hour or two."

"What sources?" Maggie demanded, her suspicion growing even stronger. "What is going on here? I insist that you tell me at once!"

"I shall leave it to Sir to make the explanations." Peter was hurrying towards the door. "He is really much better at handling such things than I. *Au revoir.*" And he closed the door behind him.

"Well?" Maggie asked in the silence that followed his departure. "I am waiting . . . *Sir.*"

He grimaced at her words. "For God's sake, Maggie, don't call me that," he muttered, casting a nervous look at the far wall. He was well aware that Miss Spenser had yet to put in an appearance, which meant she could be anywhere; including the secret passage, listening to every word.

"Why not? That is your name, isn't it?" Maggie snapped, pulling free of his hold. She felt torn in opposing directions all at once; wanting to keep him close to her, but wanting his safety even more.

"Yes, but I'd just as lief you not announce that fact to anyone who might be listening," he grumbled, reaching out to grab her hand. "Come, ma'am, if you insist upon ringing a peal over my head, then let us go outside so that you can screech at me in private." And he guided her out of the house and towards the windswept cliffs.

Maggie walked sullenly beside him. She felt like pointing out that there were fewer places more private than a deserted room, but she perversely held her tongue. But as they continued walking, her anger gave way to a deep sense of uneasiness. All her doubts and suspicions about Ian returned tenfold to plague her, and by the time they reached their destination, she was sick with a cold certainty.

"Ian, I have had enough of your prevarications and half-truths! I want the full truth, and I want it now." She turned to face him, drawing a steadying breath as she fixed him with an unwavering gaze. "Are you an agent?"

Ian lowered his head, his eyes closing with a bitter weariness. "Maggie, please, don't ask this of me," he said, his tone bleak. "I can't tell you."

"Why?" She was horrified to find herself blinking back tears. "Is it because you don't trust me?"

He raised his head at that, angry blue eyes meeting hers. "Don't you understand?" he ground out, "I *can't*. My God, do you have the smallest conception of what such an admission could mean?"

"Of course I do," she replied quietly, refusing to flinch from the raw emotions in his stormy eyes. "My father was a colonel in the guard, and I know well the dire consequences of breaching security, but I had hoped you would trust me enough to know that I would die sooner than reveal your secret to another living soul." Her lips quivered as the tears spilled out of her eyes and trailed down her cheeks. "It seems I was mistaken. You really don't trust anyone . . . do you?"

Ian felt as if he were being devoured alive, so great was his pain. He wanted to tell her, God, he wanted to, but a decade of training kept him mute. All of his instincts warned him this could be a trap; he had believed a woman once before and had almost died as a result. His dictum that one could never be too cautious had kept both him and his men safe through ten years of war, and it would not easily be set aside. And yet . . .

"The Runners aren't after me," he said at last, his voice harsh with strain. "My story about the duel was pure fabrication. But even if it were true and they did take me up, I would be released . . . eventually. That is all I can tell you."

Maggie's shoulders slumped as she accepted all he had told her, and all he had not. "Thank you," she said quietly, realizing how much it had cost him to tell her even that.

"If something untoward should happen and I am arrested," he continued, his heart pounding with the enormity of the risk he was taking, "then you are to say nothing; nothing, do you hear me? Blakely will know what to do."

"All right."

"I mean it, Maggie," he insisted, cupping her face with his hands and staring down into her eyes. "No matter what happens, you are never to reveal my identity. My reputation, my freedom, even my life, none of it matters. Do you understand?"

"Yes!" she cried, her own hands stealing up to frame his face. "For pity's sake, Ian, can't you trust me even that far?"

"I do trust you," he answered, lowering his head to hers. "God help me, but I do," and he took her mouth in a ferocious kiss.

Maggie's lips parted beneath the onslaught of his, accepting both his pain and his passion with a desperation born of love. Her hands slipped up into the gilded softness of his hair as she pressed herself against him, responding to him with a wildness that would have shocked her had she been in any state to consider the matter. For now, her mind and senses were filled with Ian, and she gave him all the love she had kept hidden for so long.

Ian felt her response, and his body clenched with hunger. He knew he should stop, knew he should call off this madness before it went any further, but he could not. After years of living for nothing more than cold duty, he found himself wanting something for himself. He wanted Maggie.

"Maggie." He groaned her name against her lips, his fingers gently stroking her breasts beneath her velvet cape. "Sweet, sweet Maggie."

"Ian." Maggie could barely speak. She felt on the edge of a precipice even higher than the one on which she stood; higher and far more dangerous. Her heart was beating so fast and hard that she was certain it would escape the confines of her chest, and her body burned with the thick blood flowing through it. In that moment she knew that she would never love any man the way she loved Ian, and she longed to express that love to him.

The high call of a sea gull broke the spell binding Ian, bringing him back painfully to a sense of time and place. He lifted his head and stared down into Maggie's flushed face, reading her passion with a sense of exultation. "Ah, my love, but what you do to a man's reason, 'tis criminal," he murmured.

She stared up at him, knowing her heart was in her eyes and not caring a whit. "Ian, I—"

"Shh." He brushed his lips over hers. "Not a word. 'Tis time we were heading back to the house. There is much we must do, and precious little time to do it in. Now, when is the dinner party?"

The rapidity with which he switched from ardent lover to cool conspirator left Maggie feeling oddly bereft, and she was strongly tempted to demand that he resume the lovemaking. Only an innate sense of modesty and the fear he would refuse kept her from doing just that, and she was proud of the steadiness of her voice as she replied, "I had planned it for next Thursday, if that meets with your approval, Captain Sherrill."

"That give us almost six days," he said, doing some rapid calculations in his mind. "If Blakely leaves tonight, he could be back with the information we need in about three days. That would be cutting it rather close, but I suppose there's no help for it."

"No help for what?" Maggie asked, wondering what was going on behind his sea blue eyes. "What are you plotting?"

He ignored her. "And I'll need another messenger to ride to Lincolnshire; Merrick should be available, and if worst comes to worst, I suppose I could send for Marchfield."

"Who are all these people?" she demanded, laying a hand on his arm. "Ian, tell me what is going on!"

He glanced down at her, his smile distant as he gave her hand a reassuring pat. "Only some friends, my love. Some friends who are going to help us catch our ghost."

"The ghost?" Maggie was beginning to wonder if something had addled her beloved's mind. "What has she to do with all of this?"

"Everything." The grin he gave her was razor-sharp. "She is going to be the trap we use to snare our villain. Now, listen carefully, Maggie, this is what you are going to do . . .

"Well, it's all rather havey-cavey if you ask me," Leonora grumbled later that night as she, Constance, and Maggie sat in the drawing room while Ian and the reverend lingered over their brandy. "First Mr. Blakely comes dashing down to Cornwall to rescue his injured friend, and not five days later he goes haring back to London without him. Not the actions of a gentleman, to my way of thinking," she added with a meaningful sniff.

"I have told you, Miss Thomas," Maggie explained as she added another stitch to the sampler she was working on. "Mr. Blakely left his best evening jacket at his London lodgings, and nothing would do but that he go and fetch it. You must have noticed he was something of a . . . er . . . dandy.'' She hesitated using the dismissing word, even though it was the very one Peter had cheerfully used to describe himself.

"A man-milliner if ever there was one,'' Leonora gloated. "It's a pity he didn't take that captain with him when he left. I am beginning to think that we may never be shed of him, Miss Chambers.''

Maggie sincerely prayed this was the case, although she held out precious little hope for it. Since their embrace on the cliffs that afternoon, Ian had gone out of his way to avoid her, and although she told herself he was only doing so to uphold his end of the plot, she was still worried. Pushing her own troubles aside, she picked up the thread of the conversation, ever mindful of Ian's instructions.

"You needn't worry about me, Miss Thomas,'' she said, jabbing her needle through the soft cotton. "I know how to rid my home of unwelcome guests.'' She paused long enough to let the other woman know she had just been insulted and then added, "I only wish I could be rid of that pesky ghost as well. I vow she is becoming a nuisance.''

Constance jerked, pricking her finger with the needle. "Do you mean to say you have seen the ghost?'' she demanded, sucking on her injured finger. "When?''

"Oh, off and on over the past week.'' Maggie shrugged her shoulders indifferently. "She has been on my balcony at least twice, and my dreams have become positively gothic. I am beginning to think I shall never know a good night's sleep again.'' She smothered a yawn behind her hand.

"I thought you were beginning to look rather peaked,'' Constance said, studying Maggie speculatively. "But why did you not say something sooner? I would be more than willing to sleep in your rooms, or you could ask Mrs. Hartcup to move you to another wing. I am sure the visitations would then stop."

"What? Allow some troublesome spirit to drive me out of that lovely room?" Maggie glowered at her. "Never. Besides, I am not all that sure it would do anything. As Miss Thomas said, the wretched thing seems to have singled me out, for some unknown reason."

"But—"

"No," Leonora interrupted, shooting Constance an angry scowl. "Miss Chambers is right. That emissary of the darker powers would only find her no matter where she chooses to lay her head, and if she is going to confront it, it is best to do it on her own ground. What are your plans, Miss Chambers?"

"I really cannot say." Mindful of her role, Maggie yawned again. "I am so exhausted, I can scarce think. If only I could sleep one night through, I am convinced everything would be all right."

"Perhaps some warm milk might help you," Constance said hesitantly. "I could ask Cook to prepare you some, if you'd like."

"Constance, the very thing!" Maggie beamed at her over the sinking of her heart. "Would you?"

"It would be my pleasure," Constance assured her with a sweet smile. "In fact, I shall do it right now. When would you like it delivered to your room?"

Maggie thought about that. Ian had said it would take him until midnight to get into position . . . whatever that meant . . . which left her less than three hours to drink the milk and then fall conveniently asleep. "Oh, shall we say in an hour, Constance?" she asked with a bright smile. "I know I

180

should stay awake and visit a while, but really, I am so tired."

"But Robert wanted me to read from the Book of Galatians," Leonora protested, her thin nose twitching with annoyance. "You can't possible hope to face that evil specter without first arming yourself with the Holy Word!"

"I shall read my own Bible in my room, Miss Thomas," Maggie replied, thinking that if she were indeed suffering from insomnia, then listening to the other woman's flat voice droning on would prove a far more effective remedy than warm milk. "You needn't concern yourself."

"But—"

"In fact, I believe I shall read Ephesians," she said brightly. "I'm sure the passage about putting on the whole armor of God ought to prove quite effective, don't you? Never fear, Miss Thomas, I shall be well guarded, I promise you." And she picked up her mending, ignoring the other woman's strident attempts to continue the conversation.

That will be all, Ann, thank you," Maggie said some two hours later, casting her maid a polite smile. "You may go now."

"Aren't you going to drink your milk, miss?" The maid's eyes flicked towards the glass of milk sitting on her bedside table. "Miss Spenser said you asked for it special."

"Yes, but I believe I'll sip it later as I read," Maggie replied, her tone cheerful despite her strong misgivings. Ann had been the one to bring her the milk before; what if she was the one who had slipped the drug in it?

After the maid left, Maggie slipped out of her bedclothes and donned one of her riding habits before climbing back into bed. Ian had told her to be dressed and ready to move in the event the ghost made its appearance, although he'd failed to tell her why. Evidently "Sir" wasn't accustomed to explaining himself, she thought sourly, shifting onto her back as she sought a more comfortable position in which to spend the next few hours.

She'd barely gotten settled when she heard a scratching noise coming from the balcony. The ghost? She lay quietly as the sound came again, and she realized she was shaking with fear. It would seem she wasn't as brave as she thought she was, she mused, gathering her courage for a quick peek. Just as she was about to turn her head, there was a sudden movement by her bed, and seconds later, a hand came crashing down over her mouth, smothering the scream she was about to utter.

"Be quiet, you little fool," Ian hissed in her ear, cautiously easing his hand from her lips. "Do you want to bring the whole house dashing in here?"

She collapsed against the pillows, glaring up at him. Her room was still in darkness, but in the faint moonlight streaming through the opened door, she could just make out his features. "You beast!" she whispered, angrily batting his hand away. "You almost frightened me to death! What are you doing here, anyway? I thought you were supposed to be getting into position."

"I am." Ian smiled at her belligerent tones. "What better place to trap your ghost?"

"You're going to spend the night in here?" Maggie was both shocked and pleased by the news. Although she knew her reputation would be forever ruined should they be discovered, she refused to dwell on the matter. It might be highly unconventional, but she knew Ian would never take advantage of the situation . . . or her.

"Please, this is hardly the time for you to turn missish on me," Ian said as he moved into the shadows. "My intentions are strictly honorable, I assure you. Is this the milk?" His fingers closed about the glass and he raised it to his lips for a cautious taste.

"Laudanum?" she asked as he spat the milk into the chamber pot.

"Or something stronger," he said, setting the glass down and stepping back into the darkness. "At least now my suspicions are confirmed. Constance definitely has an ally."

Maggie lay back against the pillows. "You're certain she is involved?" She felt strangely awkward talking to him in the intimate confines of the soft night. Would this be what it would be like if they were married? she dreamed wistfully. Would they lie in the darkness and talk quietly, perhaps touching each other with the gentleness of lovers? Her cheeks grew pleasantly warm at the thought.

"I will be once our ghost makes her appearance," Ian replied, his tone curt. He was painfully aware of the effect being in Maggie's bedchamber was having on him, and it took all of his considerable will not to join her in her maidenly bed. He shook off the erotic images that very thought invoked, concentrating instead on the reason for his presence here tonight.

Maggie heard the impatience in his voice and swallowed the rest of her questions. They waited in a tense silence as the moon climbed high in the sky, its silvery white light flooding the room, but still there was no sign of the ghost. Finally, after what seemed an eternity, Ian said, "It appears our ghostly lady had a previous engagement; I don't believe she is going to honor us with a performance."

Maggie sat up, the bedclothes tumbling to her waist. "Then perhaps it isn't Constance," she said hopefully, relieved that her companion had been proved innocent.

"She's involved." Ian's voice was grim. "I don't

know how or why, but she is involved, Maggie, never doubt that. It could mean your life."

"Oh, Ian." She shook her head at him. "Must you be so cynical? Not everyone is a villain, you—"

"Shh!" His hissed warning came seconds before the pale figure drifted into view, arms outstretched in supplication. Before Maggie could even gasp, Ian was on his feet, a pistol in his hand as he bolted out onto the balcony to confront the ghost.

Chapter Thirteen

Shock held Maggie immobile for one moment, and then she was scrambling after Ian. By the time she reached the balcony, there was no sign of either him or the ghost. She glanced wildly about her, fearing for one moment that he had somehow fallen over the parapet, and then she saw the small opening in the wall. Without pausing to weigh the danger, she plunged into the dark, narrow passage.

"Ian?" she called, her voice echoing eerily in the blackness that surrounded her like a clinging fog. "Ian, where are you?"

"Here." She heard his voice moments before she felt his hands closing on her shoulders. "I suppose it was too much to hope that you would actually obey my orders and stay in the room."

"Apparently so." She was so relieved to have him safe that she didn't feel like debating the matter, although she was compelled to add, "Not that you issued any such orders, mind you."

Ian was not amused. "Some things shouldn't have to be said," he retorted, furious that his quarry had disappeared without a trace. He'd had her in sight for a brief moment and then she'd simply vanished as if she were the ghost she pretended to be.

Without saying a word, he guided her back to her own room, making sure the door to the balcony was secured before he lit the candle at her bedside table. "That was a damned stupid thing to do," he said, his voice cutting as he turned to face her. "Didn't it occur to you that you were in danger?"

His harsh words flicked against Maggie's pride, and her own temper flared in response. "No, it didn't," she said, her chin coming up belligerently. "But it did occur to me that *you* might be. Why do you think I went dashing into that tunnel after you? And that's another thing," she added, with mounting indignation, "how long have you known that tunnel was there? Why didn't you tell me? This is my house, you know."

"Indeed I do, my lady," he replied with a mocking bow, "which is precisely why I chose not to tell you. Troublesome vixen that you are, I knew you wouldn't rest until you'd explored it, regardless of the danger to yourself and others. But now that you do know it's there, I want your word that you won't ever go into it unless Peter or I am with you."

Maggie longed to defy him, but her common sense prevented her. She knew the order was meant for her own protection, and that she would be foolish in the extreme to disobey him merely out of pique. "Oh, very well," she said, shooting him a resentful look, "I give my word. But—" she held up a warning finger "—I fully expect a complete tour once Mr. Blakely is back from London. Agreed?"

"Agreed." Ian was relieved she was being so reasonable, although he didn't expect the condition would last very long. He smiled slightly and stroked her cheek. "Thank you, Maggie."

"For what?"

His smile deepened at her distrustful tones. "For

obeying me. And for running into that tunnel after me. I'm used to operating alone and I appreciate your help, although I would prefer that you not make a habit of it. I don't think I could bear it if something were to happen to you."

Maggie's color deepened at his words, and at the glow in his eyes as he spoke them. She turned her head enough so that her lips brushed against his hand. "I feel the same," she said softly, wishing she were less a lady, and Ian less than a man of honor. "Promise me you won't take any needless risks because of me."

His thumb caressed her bottom lip, his heart contracting with pain as he realized the enormity of the risk he'd already taken on her behalf. "I won't," he said, masking his deepest emotions out of habit. He allowed himself one final touch and then stepped away, his hand dropping to his side.

"Now, try and get some sleep," he ordered, striding towards the balcony. "I'll jam the door from the other side of the passage so you needn't worry about any nocturnal visitors, and if you see or hear anything at all, I want you to scream down the house and then get the devil out of here."

"Yes, Ian." She couldn't help but smile at his brisk tones.

"I mean it." He gave her a menacing look over his broad shoulder. "And on no account are you to go out onto that balcony. The whole thing is about to come crashing down at any moment, and I don't want you out there when it does. Do you hear me?"

"Yes, Ian."

"And I want you to give Constance and Dr. Garlowe a wide berth for the next few days. On no account are you to be alone with them; especially the doctor."

Maggie was startled out of her complacency. Painful as it was, she had finally accepted Constance's involvement in the plot against her. But Dr. Garlowe? She frowned at Ian.

"Are you saying he is after me as well?" she asked, disbelief obvious in her voice. "Good heavens, Ian, I scarce know the man!"

Ian paused at the doorway, his hands on his lean hips as he confronted her. "You once said that I was wrong because I refused to trust other people," he said, his eyes resting on her face. "Now I'm asking you to show me that same kind of trust. I can't explain now, just believe that I'm doing my best for you. Please, Maggie, trust me."

Maggie met his tortured gaze, and knew she had no other choice. How could she not trust him when she had already given him her heart? "Very well, Ian," she said softly, "I trust you."

His eyes closed briefly in relief and then he opened the door, slipping soundlessly from the room.

Peter returned from London late the following afternoon, bringing two valises and a traveling trunk with him. "I simply couldn't decide which waistcoat to wear," he explained to Maggie with one of his languid smiles, "and so I brought them all. I trust you don't mind?"

"Not at all, Mr. Blakely," Maggie replied, ignoring Miss Thomas's loud sniff. Constance hadn't joined them, claiming she had the headache, and given the events of last evening, Maggie was more than willing to give her the time off. "I am grateful that you think so much of my party to want to do it such honor," she added, giving him an encouraging smile.

"Which reminds me, I say, Marcus, do you remember Drew Merrick?" He swung his blue gaze on Ian, who was sitting quietly on the settee, a teacup held in his large hand.

Ian tensed. "Merrick? I should say that I do! What is he up to these days? I hear he got himself leg-shackled to the Earl of Terrington's daughter while I was away."

"So he did," Peter agreed pleasantly. "I ran into them at Almack's the other evening, and I told them all about your carriage accident and your stay here. Well, to make short work of a rather boring story, it seems he and Lady Melanie are going to be visiting her cousins, the Fitz-Suttons, next week, and when I told them of the party in your honor, nothing would do but that they attend. I am sorry, Miss Chambers, but there was naught I could do but invite them. An earl's daughter and all."

"You needn't apologize, Mr. Blakely." Maggie was impressed at the cleverness with which he had introduced the Merricks into the party.

"Well!" Leonora gave another sniff, her lips pursing in disapproval. "Some people certainly show a sad lack of breeding these days; only imagine inviting oneself to a private party in such a common manner! Ah well." She shrugged her bony shoulders. "She is a lady, after all, and the gentry make their own rules."

The others wisely said nothing, and they got through the rest of the hour without incident. At the end of it, Peter set his teacup down and turned to Ian. "I took a second look at that high-stepping gray I was telling you about," he said brightly, "and I do believe I shall be making an offer for her. Do you think you might give me an hour of your time so that we might discuss it further? For an infantryman, you always did know your horse-flesh."

Ian agreed with alacrity, and after bidding his hostess and the others a good afternoon, he and Peter went quickly into the library. While Ian checked the passage to make sure it wasn't in use, Peter locked the door behind them. "Well?" Ian asked once he was satisfied they were secure. "What did you learn?"

"What you thought I would." Peter's expression was grim.

"Garlowe is really William Clayburt." It was a statement rather than a question as he accepted the conclusion he'd arrived at even before sending Peter to London. It all fit too neatly to be a coincidence.

Peter nodded. "Garlowe is his stepfather's name, and he uses it on occasion; without his stepfather's permission, I might add. He paid for the lad's schooling and bought him a medical commission in the army, where he promptly disgraced himself with the wife of a sergeant major."

"Constance Spenser?"

"Yes, their affair was quite the talk of Baltimore," Peter agreed sardonically. "All the more so when her husband shot himself over it."

Ian muttered an uncomplimentary remark about unfaithful wives and then asked, "Were you able to discover if he knows about the codicil to his father's will?" he asked, thrusting a hand through his dark gold hair and pacing the room.

"No, his mother denies any knowledge of it, insisting she never even told him who his real father was, and I am inclined to belive her. She seemed shocked that I knew."

"You mean you simply went to her and told her everything?" Ian exclaimed, staring at Blakely in dismay. "My God; why?"

"Because not all of us believe in doing things in your circuitous manner." Peter made no apology for his behavior. "Time was of the essence, and so I went to her and told her what I already knew and what I needed to know. She was more than happy to cooperate."

Ian cursed again, going to the window and staring out at the sea in the distance. "You realize that unless we can prove he knew of the codicil, there is nothing we can do to stop him," he said, his voice cold. "He has but to deny everything, including his parentage, and we are lost. And even if he does admit that Simington is his father, it could still spell disaster for Maggie. An illegitimate son might be considered a much more acceptable heir rather than a grand-niece once removed."

"That is so." Peter rubbed his ear absently. "Not to mention the potential scandal if we do manage to bring the bastard to justice. And since the Crown isn't involved, there will be no offering him the gentleman's way out; a favorite method of yours, or so I am told."

"It's effective," Ian retorted coolly, his mind dwelling on what Peter had just said. He was right; curse him. A trial, no matter how delicately handled, would still bring scandal down on Maggie's head; not to mention the hue and cry that would be raised if his involvement were discovered.

"The law need not be involved," he said, a plan forming in his mind. "We could go to Garlowe, tell him what we know, and offer him the choice of quietly leaving England. If he is a wise man, he'll take it."

"Especially if he knows the alternative," Peter murmured, a copper eyebrow arching in amusement. "I take it you will make it quite plain to him?"

Ian's eyes flashed with a deadly fire. "I'll make it plain to him, all right," he said, his voice soft with menace. "By the time I am done with him, Garlowe will know that remaining in England will be tantamount to signing his own death warrant."

"When do you plan on telling him?" Peter asked,

accepting Ian's violent promise without censure. "It should be soon, before another attempt is made."

"I agree, especially after last night." And he told Peter about the trap that had failed to catch the ghost.

"There could be a second passageway," Peter said when Ian described how he had lost Constance in the twisting darkness. "One that opens up off the main tunnel. That house near my father's is a veritable rabbit warren of tunnels and secret chambers, and I must say all of this is giving me an interesting idea. But for the moment, let us concentrate on the doctor and his ladylove. Shall we ride over there now? I must say I am rather looking forward to giving them both their congé."

"No more than I," Ian said, his hands tightening into fists as if in anticipation of closing around Garlowe's throat. "But it might be better if we waited until after the dinner party. They know we're suspicious, so we needn't worry they'll act hastily. In the meanwhile, we'll see if Drew can uncover anything else. The more ammunition we have to use against them, the more cooperative they're likely to be."

"Brilliant as usual, Sir." Peter inclined his head. "But what of Miss Chambers? She'll have to be told."

"I've already told her that both are our best suspects," he said, wincing at the disillusionment Maggie would feel when faced with the full knowledge of Constance's duplicity. "She's promised to avoid both of them, so at least I don't need to fear another riding 'accident.'"

"Do you think you may count upon her to keep her word?" Peter eyed Ian speculatively. "I've noticed Miss Chambers to be a rather independently minded female."

Ian smiled. "I trust her," he said softly, the truth

that had been flickering at the edge of his consciousness finally becoming a warm blaze that filled his very being. "I trust her." And in his heart he substituted the word love for trust; knowing that for him, they were the very same thing.

The day before the dinner party, the Merricks arrived to introduce themselves to Maggie and thank her for her "invitation." She found Lady Melanie to be enchantingly lovely, and not the least bit haughty despite her title and fortune. Drew Merrick was handsome in a rather masculine fashion, and there was something in his cool, watchful manner that put her strongly in mind of Ian. She mentioned this to Lady Melanie while the two of them were enjoying a quiet walk in the garden, and the other woman gave a light laugh.

"When I first met Sir, I thought he reminded me of Drew," she said, her violet eyes sparkling with remembrance. "All of Sir's men, or at least the ones I have met, are like that. Dangerous, yes, but with an underlying sense of integrity and duty. Have you met the Duke of Marchfield yet?"

"No," Maggie replied, wondering what Lady Melanie meant by Sir's men. Did she mean Ian was more than the simple spy he had more or less admitted to being?

"You will." Lady Melanie's glossy black hair shone in the sunlight as she removed her bonnet. "Drew doesn't know it, but I wrote Jacinda, the duke's wife, and told her about Sir's carriage accident. I daresay they should be here any day now. They're devoted to Sir, as are we."

"Have you known Ian . . . Sir for very long?" Maggie asked, nervously wetting her lips. Lady Melanie was the first person to speak so openly about Ian, and she ached for information about the man she loved.

"Oh, about two years." Lady Melanie's shrewd gaze rested on Maggie's face. "How long have you known you are in love with him?"

Maggie's face paled and then reddened in dismay. "I . . . I don't know what you mean, Lady Melanie," she stammered, feeling as if someone had just torn off all her clothes, leaving her exposed to the world's eyes. "We haven't known each other but for a few weeks and . . . and . . ."

"And I fell in love with Drew in about half that time." Lady Melanie covered Maggie's hand with hers. "He was posing as the butler in my father's establishment at the time, so you may imagine my consternation. Come, Miss Chambers, if I have learned anything in my years with Drew, it is that life is far too short and uncertain to waste with false pride. Do you love Sir?"

Tears gathered in Maggie's eyes as she finally confessed the truth. "Yes," she whispered, oddly relieved to be speaking the words out loud. "I do love him, more than I can tell you, but I fear it will do me little good."

Lady Melanie was silent, giving Maggie time to compose herself before she said, "Sir is not an easy man to know; we have been acquainted all these years, and I still can think of him only as Sir. I didn't even know his real name until some months ago, and then Drew swore me to secrecy. You do know about Sir's . . . er . . . avocation?" She gave Maggie a sharp look.

Maggie smiled at the other woman's careful choice of words. "He has told me nothing," she admitted, wiping the tears from her cheeks, "but I would have to be a fool not to know there is more to Ian than a scandalous name and a propensity for disguises. He was posing as a Captain Sherrill when we first met," she added by way of explanation.

"So I have heard," Lady Melanie replied with a

laugh. You must know he is the best kept secret in England."

Maggie swallowed uncomfortably. "I know he must be . . . careful." She hesitated over the right word. "He doesn't seem to trust many people."

"And with good cause," Lady Melanie said, casting Maggie a worried look. "I don't know all the details, but Drew says there was a lady . . . a Frenchwoman whom Sir loved very much, and she betrayed him to the soldiers. He was imprisoned and tortured, and it was only through his own courage that he managed to escape. After so harsh a lesson, is it any wonder that he is so reluctant to trust?"

"He trusts me," Maggie said, her heart contracting at the thought of what Ian must have suffered.

"Does he?" Lady Melanie's expression grew thoughtful. "Then he must love you, for I cannot imagine Sir saying that to any woman unless he cared very deeply. You mustn't give up hope, my dear," she said, giving Maggie's hand a gentle squeeze. "Men like Sir, like my Drew, are not easily won, but they are well worth it in the end. You'll see."

This conversation was uppermost in Maggie's mind the next evening as she dressed for her first dinner party as mistress of Bride's Leap. She wore a dress of gold silk trimmed with green ribbons, her fiery-colored hair arranged in a sophisticated riot of curls. Emeralds that had once belonged to her great-great-grandmother circled her throat, and she thought that she looked quite regal. Dabbing a bit of perfume at her wrists, she smiled wistfully, wondering what Ian would think when he saw her in her finery.

She'd scarce seen him since the night he had chased the ghost from her room, and had it not been for the lambent glow in his eyes whenever he looked at her, she would have been quite sunk with unhappiness. He and Mr. Blakely had spent hours closeted away with Mr. Merrick, emerging from the library looking grimly determined. Something was definitely afoot, and she wondered sourly if she'd ever know what it was.

She was just debating whether or not she should resort to the rouge pot when Constance entered the room, attired in a stunning gown of blue and silver satin. "Good evening, Miss Chambers," she said, looking as angelically sweet as always. "How lovely you look; every inch the mistress of the manor."

"Thank you, Constance." It took all of Maggie's control to keep the revulsion out of her voice, and her smile was strained as she turned to face the other girl. "How are you feeling this evening? Is your headache finally gone?" Her bogus companion had been hiding in her room, claiming she was suffering from a vicious migraine.

"Oh yes." Constance seemed unaware of the faint challenge in Maggie's voice. "I am quite recovered, I promise you. And thank you for being so kind about my indisposition; I am sure not many employers would be so understanding."

"You're welcome, Constance." Maggie picked up her gold and green plumed fan from the dressing table and rose to her feet, a false smile pinned to her lips. "Well, shall we go down and greet our guests?" she asked brightly. "The evening awaits."

Ian was standing at the base of the stairs, and at the sight of her, his eyes turned a deep blue. "Good evening, ma'am," he said, stepping forward to greet her with a low bow. "You do Bride's Leap proud."

"Thank you." Maggie found it hard to speak as his lips brushed over the back of her hand. He was dressed in an evening jacket of midnight blue velvet, a starched cravat at his throat, and his muscular legs encased in a pair of cream-colored evening breeches. She'd never seen him looking so handsome, and her breath caught in her throat as she offered him a tentative smile.

For a moment, everything else faded away, leaving just the two of them in the center of the universe. Her eyes met his, and in that instant she thought she could read his heart in his eyes, and for the first time, she dared hope that he returned her love. Then Peter came up to join them, and the moment was lost.

"Well, Miss Chambers, what do you think?" He held out his arms to his sides and preened like a young girl before her first ball. "Do you think I have made the right choice? Be honest now, there is still time for me to change if you do not approve."

Maggie smiled at his antics. "The waistcoat is stunning," she assured him, her eyes lingering briefly on the brightly patterned waistcoat of purple, gold, and red brocade. "How wise of you to wear it with such subdued colors."

Peter brushed a hand over the bright red satin evening jacket he was wearing. "It does clash quite dreadfully with my hair, doesn't it?" he said, sounding pleased. "And the yellow pantaloons are just the thing, don't you think? I daresay these country bumpkins have never seen the like."

"I'm sure no one has ever seen the like, God be thanked," Ian said, growing impatient to steal a few minutes with Maggie. He'd seen precious little of her during these last days, and he was anxious to speak with her.

After muttering his excuses to Constance and Peter, he dragged Maggie into the salon where she would be formally receiving her guests. After closing the door, he turned to her, his expression serious as he said, "We have enough evidence to have Garlowe and your companion transported," he began without preamble, ignoring her gasp of shock. "He is your great-uncle's illegitimate son, and she is his mistress. It is almost a certainty they have been planning your death since the moment you were named Simington's heir, and that they were both involved in the attack on you at the inn."

The blood rushed from Maggie's face, along with the joy she'd been feeling at the approaching party. It was one thing to admit intellectually that the woman she had always treated as more a friend than an employee had betrayed that friendship, she realized, blinking back tears, and quite another to have it confirmed so cruelly. She took a shuddering breath, willing herself not to cry.

"It would seem you were right, Ian," she said, her voice shaking dangerously. "Betrayal can come from anywhere."

"No." He shook his blond head, hating the cynicism he heard creeping into her tone. "I was wrong. It is foolish to judge the world so harshly."

She was too distressed to wonder at his abrupt change of heart. "And Dr. Garlowe . . . or whatever his name is, why didn't he simply come forward and claim the fortune when Great-Uncle died? I never even wanted it, and certainly he is more entitled to it than I!"

"I'll ask him when I have the chance." Ian heard the sound of laughter in the hallway and knew his time with Maggie had just run out. Cursing his lack of time, he bent his head and pressed a hard kiss on her mouth. "Keep where either Peter or I can see you," he warned, his voice urgent as guests began arriving. "I'll explain later." And then he was gone, melting away as the laughing throng of people began filing into the salon.

Chapter Fourteen

Four hours later, Maggie was standing on the terrace just off the conservatory, her eyes closing in relief as she drank in the cool night air blowing off the sea. Inside, her guests were laughing and dancing, enjoying the lively music being provided by the quartet she had hired for the evening. The ancient house rang with music and sounds of merrymaking, and while she was pleased that her first attempt at entertaining was so successful, she couldn't help but feel saddened. The party had been Ian's excuse for remaining at Bride's Leap; now that it was over, there was no reason for him to stay.

"Good evening to you, Miss Chambers." A gruff voice broke Maggie's reverie, and she turned around to find Squire Varney standing beside her, a cheroot held between his thick fingers.

"Hope you don't mind if I stand here and blow a cloud," he said, shifting from one foot to another like a schoolboy being called before the headmaster. "Elinore won't let me smoke 'em at home, don't you know."

"Please, you must make yourself comfortable," Maggie replied, momentarily diverted by the sulky pout forming on the squire's jowly countenance. She was just as shocked as everyone else when the squire and his tiny wife made their appearance just before dinner. It had taken some last-minute juggling to rearrange the table settings, but fortunately, Hartcup was more than equal to the challenge.

"Nice dinner party," the squire said, awkwardly lighting his illicit cigar. "Never thought the time would come when I'd be breaking bread here, but there you are. Thirty-one years is a long time to bear a grudge, and as I told my Elinore, 'tis not as if you had aught to do with the old ... with your great-uncle's racketing ways." He shot her an anxious look. "All ancient history, what? And better left that way, to my mind."

Maggie stirred in interest, remembering all Mrs. Hartcup had told her. Ian had said that there was enough evidence to transport Dr. Garlowe and Constance, but surely it wouldn't hurt to learn as much as was possible. What was it Ian was always saying? Ah yes, she smiled suddenly; one could never be *too* cautious.

"Yes, I have heard of the deplorable way in which Uncle Ellsworth treated your poor governess," she said with as much sangfroid as she could muster. "And I must say I am deeply shocked and ashamed that a member of my family should conduct himself so reprehensibly. I only wonder that the doctor didn't step forward and claim his rightful inheritance when my uncle passed away."

The squire choked on a mouthful of smoke, his face turning an alarming shade of red. "Do you mean you *know* about William?" he wheezed, his eyes tearing from his vigorous coughing. "Good God; how?"

Maggie hid a victorious smile. She'd been shooting blind, taking a risk that the squire was aware of the doctor's parentage, and she was smugly pleased her instincts had paid off so handsomely. She couldn't wait to see Ian's face when she told him of this latest development, she thought, trying to think of some plausible answer to give the squire.

"I was told in strictest confidence," she answered after a thoughtful pause. "I am sure you can understand why I shouldn't wish the matter bandied about."

"Aye." The older man gave a sage nod. "That would be a pretty kettle of fish, and make no doubt about it. Well, you may depend upon my discretion, Miss Chambers," he said, drawing himself up proudly. "Reckon I know when to keep my tongue between my teeth, what?"

"That is very kind of you, sir, thank you." She inclined her head graciously. "But may I ask how you knew of his identity? I was told it was a closely guarded secret."

The squire gave a furtive look about, as if suspecting an enemy spy of lurking in the rose bushes. "Always made a point to keep in contact with Helene, don't you see?" he said in a conspiratorial whisper. "When he had that spot of trouble in America, she wrote and asked if I could help the lad out. Our own doctor had just died and we had need of a physician, so I saw to it he was offered the post. Rather provident, don't you think?"

"Indeed." Maggie chewed her lower lip thoughtfully, wishing Ian were there to advise her. She didn't want to arouse the squire's suspicions by asking too many questions, but on the other hand, she didn't want to quit when she was so close to learning something of real value. Deciding she had nothing to lose and everything to gain, she took one last gamble.

"I have often thought that I should share part of my inheritance with Dr. Garlowe," she said, selecting her words with caution. "He is Uncle's son, after all, and I cannot feel it fair that he should be cut off so completely. Do you think I should tell him? About Uncle, I mean?"

"As to that, he already knows, Miss Chambers." Maggie's gamble was rewarded by the squire's confession. "I told him myself after the old goat had passed on, and you could tell he was deeply shocked by it."

"Then why didn't he contest the will?"

"What? And announce to all the world that he was a bastard?" Squire Varney shook his head. "Not likely. Besides, from the way your uncle's will was written, it wouldn't have done him a whit of good. *Legitimate* heirs, the will said, and son or nay, the doctor couldn't lay claim to that virtue. What could he do?"

What indeed? Maggie thought, anxious to rejoin the others so that she could corner Ian and tell him all she'd learned. "Yes, I can see your point," she said, fixing a bright smile on her lips, "and naturally I shall be careful not to arouse any talk. Perhaps a small annuity, don't you think? Enough to keep him in comfort but not so much as to arouse any untoward suspicions."

"Aye, that would be rare generous of you, Miss Chambers," Squire Varney approved with a hearty smile. "And it would also safeguard your own position, if you take my meaning. Although I doubt the lad would challenge you for a penny. You are the heiress by law, and so long as you live, there is naught he can do. But enough of this; I daresay 'tis time we was joining the others, Miss Chambers." And he offered her his arm, leading her back into the crowded conservatory.

Maggie spent the next hour trying to corner Ian,

but as determinedly as she stalked him, so he determinedly avoided her. If she started towards the group she was speaking with, he would adroitly slip away, and no amount of speaking glances and jerks of the head would induce him to come a step closer. She was just about to let discretion go hang and yell across the floor at him when Lady Melanie appeared at her elbow.

"You mustn't mind Sir," she said, smiling as she handed Maggie a long-stemmed glass of champagne. "He is busy reconnoitering, and I doubt he will risk public contact with you. It is his way to be twice as cautious as most men, which is why he has managed to survive this far, I suppose."

"But I am his hostess," Maggie complained, taking a mouthful of icy wine. "Surely it wouldn't arouse anyone's suspicions if he danced with me! Besides—" she took another sip "—there is something I must tell him."

"He has already danced with you twice," Lady Melanie reminded her, her lips twitching in amusement at Maggie's bellicose tones. "He can't ask you again without raising more than a few eyebrows."

Maggie muttered something under her breath about the inconvenience of conventions, her gray eyes following Ian's progress as he made his way around the room. "Well, then, why can't he sit out a dance with me? Or does he think that will cause talk, too?" she demanded, draining her glass in a noisy gulp. She didn't normally imbibe so deeply, but the room was so oppressively hot that she felt in need of refreshment. Besides, she thought darkly, accepting a second glass from the footman, this had been a trying day and she deserved to enjoy herself.

Before Lady Melanie could answer, Maggie was claimed for a dance by the eldest son of the vicar, and by the time she returned to her corner, the small brunette was waltzing with her handsome husband. Maggie consoled herself with the champagne remaining in her glass, promising that come tomorrow, she would corner Ian and tell him everything she had learned; even if it meant she had to sit upon him to do it!

By evening's end, Maggie's senses were swimming somewhat nicely, and she had to rely on Constance's help to guide her up the stairs. Ian was nowhere to be found, of course, and she felt a giddy sense of defiance when she turned to wish her treacherous companion a pleasant good night. Let him warn and threaten her all he liked, she thought, staggering slightly as she entered her room. From now on, she was going to do as she liked, and if Sir didn't like it . . . good!

Ann was waiting for her, expressing shock and disapproval at her mistress's state. "Nonsense, Ann," Maggie informed her imperiously, yawning hugely as she collapsed against the pillows. "I'm not the least bit bosky! I only had a bit of sherry before dinner and some champagne afterwards. Two glasses." She waggled her fingers in emphasis. "See? Not bosky at all."

"So my pa would say when he was in his cups," Ann grumbled, pulling the covers up over Maggie. "You'll have a fine head tomorrow, miss, mark my words, and then you'll be singing a different tune."

Singing sounded somewhat difficult to Maggie just then, as did thinking, and she closed her eyes, slipping quietly into the swirling blackness that surrounded her.

She came awake several hours later, her heart beating frantically as if she had been in a race. What on earth . . . She lifted her head from the pillow and stared groggily about the darkened room. The door to the balcony stood open, and the rain-scented breeze that was blowing made the shirred curtains billow and snap like a sail at sea. She tensed in automatic alarm, ready to flee at the first sign of the ghost, and then she saw the taller shape of a man walking towards her. Ian, she thought, her shoulders relaxing in relief. She might have known he would approach her in so stealthy a fashion.

"Really, Ian," she said, pulling the bedclothes up to her shoulders, "must you insist upon all these theatrics? Why can't you come through the door like a normal—" Her voice stopped abruptly as the pale moonlight fell across the man's face, illuminating his features.

"Not a word, not a single word, Miss Chambers," Dr. Garlowe said softly, aiming the pistol he carried at Maggie's head. "Now get up, carefully," he warned at her jerky movements, "if you think I'll hesitate using this, then you're sadly mistaken."

Maggie did as he commanded, her mind working furiously as she crawled out of bed. Think, she told herself, ignoring the terror that threatened to overwhelm her senses. There was a way out of this; there had to be. All she had to do was stay calm, and wait for a chance to escape.

"That's it." Dr. Garlowe gestured with his gun, stepping aside as Maggie walked past him and onto the balcony. Once again the secret door was open, and her heart plunged to her toes when she saw Constance standing there, a second pistol held awkwardly in her hands.

"Hello, Constance, I might have known you would be here," she said, her voice cool as she glared at her erstwhile companion. Up until now, she had been hoping against all hope that they had been wrong about Constance, and the cruelty of the other woman's betrayal cut her to the very heart.

"That's enough," Dr. Garlowe snapped, hurrying to join his mistress in the entrance to the passageway. "We've wasted enough time as it is. You have proven to be something of a nuisance, Miss Chambers. Who would have thought one little spinster should be so damned hard to kill?"

Maggie's chin came up proudly. "Did you really think I would make it easy for you?" she asked, weighing her chances for making it back into her bedroom. Although both her enemies were armed, each pistol held only one bullet, and if she was lucky, neither was a crack shot. She began edging cautiously to the side, ready to make a run for it at the first opportunity.

"One can always hope." The doctor's lips twisted in a bitter smile. "I almost had you at the inn; if it hadn't been for that damned Charles, I'd now be the master of Bride's Leap."

The thought of Ian filled Maggie with renewed courage. She hadn't let herself think of him until now, knowing she couldn't afford to be distracted for a single second. But now her love for him filled her with glowing hope and the determination to survive. Drawing on that love, she fixed them with a cool stare.

"Killing me won't avail you of my uncle's fortune," she informed them coolly. "And as for Ian, he knows all about you. He'll see you hang for what you've done."

"Do you honestly believe that with his reputation, anyone will pay him the slightest mind?" Dr. Garlowe sneered contemptuously. "The man is a byword for all that is wicked and evil, while my reputation is impeccable. Oh no, my dear Miss Chambers, after your unfortunate little accident, there is nothing that will stop me from taking what is mine."

"Unfortunate accident?" Maggie repeated, hedging desperately for time. She was aware of the shifting floor beneath her bare feet, and over the pounding of her heart, she could hear an ominous groaning sound from the stone buttress holding the balcony. "What do you mean? You're mad if you think I'll simply jump into the sea. I shall fight you with every breath in my body!"

"How melodramatic, to be sure," he said with a mocking laugh. "But you needn't think I would resort to so gothic a ploy. That was my intention at first, I grant you, but now I see that it will not do. The ghost might deceive simple country folk, but as a defense, it is somewhat chancy. Nor would your provident leap serve, unfortunately. Too many unanswered questions, you see, and in the event your paramour managed to gain a sympathetic ear, it could prove most awkward."

"Then what do you intend to do?" The audible groan Maggie heard was no figment of her imagination, and she realized to her horror that the balcony was beginning to separate from the outer wall.

"Why, nothing, Miss Chambers." The smile on Dr. Garlowe's face was the very embodiment of evil. "But you, my dear, are going to die: killed in a tragic accident when the balcony you were warned was dangerous collapses beneath your feet."

Ian came awake in an instant, all his senses fully alert as he dove out of bed, the pistol he kept hidden beneath his pillow already in his hands as he rolled to his feet. A quick glance around the darkened room revealed no obvious threat, but there was no ignoring the sense of danger that flooded his being. Something was wrong, he realized bleakly; very, very wrong.

Maggie! Ian stiffened in horror and then he was moving, barely pausing long enough to pull on some clothes. He didn't bother questioning his instincts; they had stood him in good stead over the years, and he had learned the folly of ignoring their clarion warning. He stuck another pistol into the waistband of his trousers and slid the familiar stiletto up his sleeve for good measure before slipping soundlessly out of his room and into the corridor.

His first thought was to make use of the secret tunnel; a notion he quickly discarded after a moment's consideration. The passage was too narrow to make a good defense possible, and he didn't relish the thought of being trapped in its twisting, turning maze. There was also the distinct possibility that the doctor and his lovely accomplice were already inside, and would hear him however stealthily he approached them.

Keeping to the shadows, he quickly made his way to Maggie's room, pushing open the door with the palm of his hand.

He could see Maggie clearly in the moonlight, her expression proud as she faced her enemy. Her voice was cool, and he had to strain to catch the words as he crept closer.

"A very clever plan, Doctor," Maggie said, her legs trembling with fear despite her defiant stare. "But I have only to scream to bring the household running, nor am I all that convinced you'll use your gun. A bullet wound would be rather difficult to explain, would it not?"

"You've obviously never seen a body crushed beneath a half ton or more of solid stone, Miss Chambers, or you wouldn't ask such a foolish question," Dr. Garlowe replied with a cruel laugh. "It will be difficult enough identifying what's left of you; no one would even notice another wound, I promise you."

The balcony gave another groan, and pitched wildly. Maggie staggered, and as she attempted to regain her footing, she glanced towards her room, her heart giving a convulsive leap of joy when she saw Ian standing there. For the briefest of moments their eyes and hearts met, and in that instant Maggie knew she would live. She had to; for Ian.

Ian's hand shook as emotion washed over him. So this was love, he mused, gesturing with his hand for Maggie to stand back from the line of fire. He had never felt such joy and such utter terror. The thought of Maggie in danger made him vulnerable in a dangerous way, and he refused to consider for even one moment what he would do if he was unable to save her. Calling upon a decade of fighting his way out of the most helpless of situations, he leapt forward, firing at the door to the secret passage at the same moment he reached for Maggie.

"Now!" he roared, and his arms closed around her as she leapt towards him. He savored her warmth for a brief second and then set her aside, his face dark with murderous fury as he pulled the second gun from his waistband.

"The game is up, Garlowe," he called, carefully keeping in the shadows of the room. He could see Constance on the ground, cradling her arm and crying, and cursed that the bullet hadn't struck the doctor instead. "Surrender while you still can."

"It's mine!" Garlowe shrieked, his face twisting with hatred. "It's all mine, damn you! I won't let you take it from me!" And he started forward, ignoring Constance's terrified cry.

"William, no!"

Ian raised his gun defensively, but even as he drew back the hammer, there was a loud groan as the balcony pulled free of the wall, stone and mortar crumbling into nothingness. Maggie saw the look of pure terror on the doctor's face and then he was gone, disappearing into the darkness with a high, terrified scream.

"Are you certain you're all right?" Lady Melanie asked, her violet eyes dark with concern as she gazed at Maggie's ashen face. "I can ring for some tea if you'd like."

"No, thank you, my lady," Maggie replied dully, unable to summon up so much as a smile for the other woman. It was late the next morning, and after an almost sleepless night, she was feeling decidedly the worse for wear. The intervening hours were a confused jumble in her mind; although she could vaguely remember the hullabaloo raised by the other guests who had come dashing into her room at the disturbance.

Ian had been very much the man in command, issuing orders with such authority that not even Miss Thomas dared challenge him. After turning her over to Peter for safekeeping, he'd disappeared, and she hadn't caught so much as a glimpse of him since. She was almost convinced he had already left Bride's Leap when Lady Melanie had appeared in her room, explaining gently that "Sir" wanted to speak with her.

"I'm sure Sir will be along shortly," Lady Melanie said, instinctively understanding the cause of Maggie's distress. "Drew received a message this morning and needs to speak with him. It is something you had best get used to if you mean to marry Sir. The organization is very important to him, you know."

Maggie gave a convulsive start, staring at the lovely Melanie with shock. "But I . . . but he hasn't . . . I'm not marrying Ian!" she exclaimed in confusion. "I'm not at all certain he even loves me!"

"He does." Lady Melanie's lips curved in a knowing smile. "I took one look at him and knew he was in love. And I must say 'tis about time! Jacinda and I were beginning to despair he would ever find a woman strong enough to love him. You do love him?" She regarded Maggie anxiously.

"Of course, but I—"

"Then it will all work out," Lady Melanie interrupted, laying a comforting hand over Maggie's. "Sir isn't the sort of man to let the woman he loves slip away. If he hasn't declared himself yet, he will. But you must be patient with him; he's rather new to this love business, and he's bound to be feeling all at sea."

Less than five minutes later, Ian and Drew joined the ladies, their expressions grim. "We've recovered Garlowe's body," Drew said, taking his place beside his wife. "We're putting it out that it was all a terrible accident, and with any luck, we'll be able to avoid a scandal."

"What about Constance?" Maggie asked, studying Ian's face for some clue as to his emotions. He seemed so cold, so unapproachable, not at all like the man who held her in his arms, pressing urgent kisses on her forehead. "Aren't you afraid she'll talk?"

"Not if she knows what's good for her," Drew replied, sounding every bit as commanding as Ian. "We explained very carefully to her that if she doesn't agree to leave England immediately, we'll see to it she is clapped in prison for her part in the conspiracy. I think we may count upon her to use her good sense," he added cynically.

There was an uncomfortable pause in the room as neither Maggie nor Ian could think of anything to say. Finally Lady Melanie rose to her feet, pulling her husband up with her. "All this talk of prisons is giving me a headache," she announced, prodding him towards the door. "I think a walk in the gardens is just the restorative I need; come, Drew."

The younger man obeyed docilely, a knowing gleam in his hazel eyes as he followed his wife from the room. He saw the look on Sir's face and recognized it all too well. Melanie was right, he thought, his lips curving in a complacent smile. It would be interesting to see if Sir proved as proficient at love as he was at war.

In the silence left by the Merricks' departure, Ian and Maggie continued staring at each other, each too tongue-tied and uncertain to risk speech. Finally Ian drew a deep breath, his sea blue eyes blazing with emotion as he said, "Maggie, I will be leaving with Merrick when they go."

"I . . . I see," Maggie managed, her heart beginning to pound with painful intensity. She'd been hoping for a declaration of love, and her disappointment was twice as keen. But she wasn't surprised. Somehow she'd always known Ian would leave. "May I ask where you're going? London?"

"At first," Ian admitted, wishing he could be more forthcoming. "But after that, I'm afraid I can't tell you. You do understand?" He glanced up at her anxiously, the anguish evident in the harsh lines carved into his face.

"Yes."

"It's not that I don't trust you," he rushed to say, rising to his feet to pace the confines of the study. "I do, but there is talk in the air that all is not well, and I am needed in London." He stopped in front of her, gazing down at her bent head, his eyes glowing with the love he was longing to express. "I'm sorry."

Maggie glanced up at him, catching the look on his face. "It's all right, Ian," she said softly, holding her hand out to him. All her doubts fell away, and she knew there was nothing left to fear. Casting aside all maidenly restraint, she gave him a smile that contained the full measure of her love. "Only promise me that you'll come back to me when you can. I love you."

Ian closed his eyes, relief flooding his blood. "I love you, too," he whispered, his voice husky with passion. He opened his eyes, his hands grasping hers and pulling her into his arms. "I love you," he repeated, and then his lips took hers in a kiss that contained the full weight of that love.

Maggie returned it tenfold, opening herself up eagerly for his caress. This was heaven, she thought, cupping Ian's head with her hands and pressing closer. This was everything she had ever dreamed of, and so much more.

Ian wanted to continue touching her, but his good sense overrode his desires, and he set her carefully away from him. Kissing her hand, he led her to the settee set before the fire, settling her on his lap as he sat down.

"It won't be easy," he said quietly, stroking her hair as he stared into the hypnotic dance of the flames. "All else aside, there is the not so little matter of my reputation to be considered. It will have to stand as it is." He bent his head and gave her an anxious look. "Do you think you could bear life married to a man many will label a rake and a fortune hunter?"

Maggie kissed the worried expression from his face. "So long as that rake is you, yes," she said softly, her eyes beginning to dance with some of their customary devilry. "Besides, who else is a nouveau riche companion supposed to marry but an impoverished lord down on his luck?"

Ian chuckled softly. "I hadn't thought of it in quite that light before," he said ruefully. "But just to set your own mind at ease, I do have some money. Not as much as you, of course, but enough to see us comfortably. I might bear the name, my love, but I'd as lief not live the role."

Maggie's kiss convinced him she was more than agreeable to his plan, and when Ian next raised his head, his blue eyes were serious. "There is something I want you to have," he said, digging into his pocket and extracting the miniature he had carried with him for more than a decade. He handed it to Maggie, his eyes intent upon her face.

Maggie turned it over in her hands, tears gathering in her eyes as she studied the other woman's painted features. "I ... I don't understand," she stammered, raising confused eyes to Ian's face. "This is your miniature of Lynette."

"I know," Ian replied, feeling as if a heavy weight had rolled from his chest. For the first time in his life, he felt truly free, and he struggled for the words to explain his feelings to Maggie.

"I was twenty-four when that was painted," he began, knowing only the truth would serve between them. "And I was wildly in love with her in the manner of all young men. Even then I was working for the Crown, albeit as a very junior courier, and I was foolish enough to confide in Lynette about a particular mission.

"It wasn't supposed to be all that dangerous, and so when Lynette insisted she come along, I could see no harm in it. She spoke French, after all, and said she knew the area I'd been ordered to survey. The soldiers were waiting when we landed, and while they carted me off trussed up like a Christmas goose, I could hear Lynette laughing as she counted the gold they were giving her."

Maggie flinched at his words, and at his quiet tone as he relived what had to be the most painful moment in his life. Her arms tightened protectively about him as if she would guard against further pain. "Oh, Ian, I am so sorry," she whispered, her eyes misting with tears at the thought of what he had endured.

"I was imprisoned in an isolated villa and tortured," he continued in the same calm voice. "But I managed to live ... somehow, and even escaped the night my jailers grew careless. I reached our

214

contact in Lyons and was smuggled back into England, more or less alive.

"I can't tell you what I was like those first few months after my escape. I drank too much, gambled too much, and did everything I could to earn the reputation I now bear. Sometimes, when I was deep in my cups, I'd take out the portrait of Lynette and curse all women for their perfidity." He closed his eyes at the memory of that time when he had courted death and disgrace with a bitter disregard for the consequences.

"Eventually I pulled myself back together and resumed my work, but I was not the innocent, starry-eyed lad I'd been. I became Sir, the perfect spy, consumed with nothing but revenge and the determination never to trust again." His hands cupped Maggie's face, turning it up to his as he traced her full lip with the pad of his thumb.

"When I first saw you, I was recovering from a wound I received in ambush when one of my men betrayed me," he said softly. "My superiors ordered me to take a holiday, and I was feeling resentful and bitter. Spying was all I knew, it was my life, and without it, I felt as helpless as a ship without a rudder. I was intrigued by you, and when you were attacked, I saw it as just another duty to see you safely home. At least—" his lips twisted in a rueful smile "—that is what I told myself at the time."

"And now?" Maggie turned her head to kiss his hand, savoring his salty taste.

"Now I know that I loved you from the first," he admitted, pressing a kiss on her soft mouth. "For so many years I had been a dead man inside, only going through the motions of living because I was too afraid to let myself trust again. You made me feel things I thought I'd never feel again, and even when I cursed you for the effect you had on me, I was drawn ever closer. Don't leave me, Maggie," he added on a sudden, desperate note, his hands clenching painfully around her. "For then I would truly be a dead man walking. I couldn't live without you."

"Nor I without you," Maggie told him after another exchange of fiery kisses. "I won't try and stop you from doing what you must, but at least promise me you'll be careful. I do love you so dreadfully."

"I'll be careful," he promised her, his eyes glowing with love. "Now that I have something to live for, you may rest assured that I'll be as careful with my skin as a young girl."

They continued with their lovemaking and only drew apart when Ian felt his control slipping again. "What do you want me to do with this?" Maggie asked, her voice somewhat breathless with passion. It was hard to think, but she forced herself to be sensible.

"Whatever you like," Ian replied, tucking a strand of hair behind her ear. "I have you now, and I no longer need Lynette. She has held me in her toils long enough, and 'tis time I was shed of her."

Maggie's heart grew heavy with love as she realized all Ian was telling her. She gazed up into his eyes, and reading the love and trust there, she knew what she had to do. She handed the miniature back to Ian.

"It is yours," she said, meeting his gaze unflinchingly. "Lynette was your past, and you must deal with it."

Ian gazed down at the smiling portrait of the beautiful, treacherous woman he had loved as a lad, and then into the features of the woman he now loved as a man. "You're right," he said, loving her for her wisdom and her strength. "Lynette is my past, and you are my future. I no longer need her now. I have you." And he tossed the portrait into the fire, not even looking as it was consumed by the greedy flames.

They resumed kissing, lost in passion until they heard an outraged gasp behind them.

"Well!" Miss Thomas stood there, her lips pursed in a thin line. "So this is how you mean to conduct yourself!" she shrieked. "You are a . . . a wanton! The veriest hussy! And I shall see that all of England knows you for the evil woman that you are! See if I do not."

"See here, Miss Thomas." Ian put Maggie aside and rose to his feet, his face set in a menacing scowl. "Miss Chambers is soon to be my wife, and I'll not have you talk about her that way. If you value your skin, you'll mind that viper's tongue of yours."

But Leonora was in high dudgeon and refused to be intimidated. "I shall shout her infamy from the highest steeple," she continued dramatically, "I'll—"

"Leonora," a deep masculine voice sounded from the doorway, and Ian and Maggie both turned in surprise to see Brother Thomas standing there, glaring at his sister with narrowed eyes. Both Ian and Maggie exchanged startled looks, for this was the first time either had ever heard him speak.

He advanced into the room, bearing down on his sister like an avenging angel. Leonora retreated before him, her mouth opening and closing as she sputtered.

"But . . . but, Richard, she—"

"Shut up." The reverend spoke the words with the cool finality of a judge passing sentence, his hands on the lapels of his black frock coat. When he was satisfied with the results of his handiwork, he cast a glance to the corner where Ian and Maggie were gaping at him in utter shock. He gave them both a beatific smile and drew himself upright. "When's tea?"

*R*egency...

HISTORICAL
ROMANCE
AT ITS FINEST